West Wind

When Love Speaks

Contemporary Romance, Book Three

ROBIN VAN AUKEN

Hands on Heritage LLC
589 Sylvan Dell Park Road
South Williamsport, PA 17701

ISBN-13: 978-0-9898505-0-6

Printed in the United States of America

DEDICATION

For Lance

WHEN LOVE SPEAKS

Many can brook the weather that love not the wind.

— William Shakespeare, Love's Labour's Lost

CHAPTER ONE

James Weaver tilted a brass watering can over the small garden at his property line. "No, I haven't seen her today," he said to his wife. "How am I supposed to know if she's okay?"

Ida Weaver stood on their neighbor's front porch, where she alternately rang the bell, knocked on the door and tapped on the window.

"Well, she never goes anywhere," Ida said, keeping her voice low so the elderly woman inside wouldn't hear. "She hasn't driven the Cadillac for at least a month."

"Just try the door then. I doubt it's locked." His sage advice delivered, James went back to tending his flowers.

Ida visited Rose Windham a few times a week, getting as close as any neighbor could to the reclusive old lady. It was mid-morning, so Rose shouldn't be in bed. Ida hesitated, then twisted the knob and opened the door of the Victorian mansion.

James dropped the watering can on his toe at the sound of her scream.

* * *

Sabrina's heart pounded as she groped for the telephone.

"Sabrina?" Her mother's husky voice still carried a slight Portuguese accent. "Are you awake?"

"I am now," she said, swinging her legs off the side of the bed. "What's wrong? Is Daddy okay?"

"Yes, he's fine. It's Grandmother Rose."

"What's happened?" Sabrina rubbed her face, wiping sleep from her heavy lids.

"She's in the hospital. She fell. Daddy's on the cell phone with her neighbor now. Doctors say she may have had a stroke."

Sabrina had limited experience with illness. Her parents were healthy and Rose seemed invincible. These three made up her small family.

"We need you to go to Eaton."

Sabrina exhaled. Here it came. "Isn't Daddy going?"

"We're leaving for Tibet in two days, Sabrina. We can't change our plans now. We have our visas and tickets. Our itinerary isn't flexible." Her mother's voice rose, no longer husky.

Sabrina heard the threat of tears. She wondered if they were for Grandmother Rose, unconscious in a hospital on the East Coast, or if they were for Marta, herself, busy planning yet another trip to the Orient.

Her parents, Norman and Marta Windham, were bohemian writers, renowned more for their eccentric personalities and fantastic destinations than for the quality of the books they wrote as a team. For more than twenty years, their popular series of "Tread Lightly" travel guides sold well. They wrote about backpacking the Himalayas, rafting the Amazon, floating across Africa in a hot air balloon, and snowshoeing through British Columbia. They retained the "eco-friendly" attitude that attracted them to each other as young college students, sipping green tea, dining on hummus and lentils, favoring Birkenstock shoes and all-cotton clothing.

As the daughter of aging hippies who smoked who-knows-what in their Hookah, Sabrina mutinied in her youth. At the age of eleven, fighting her way out of a lifestyle embellished with the exotic artifacts of her parents' travels, Sabrina begged to enroll in an all-girl, Catholic preparatory school in Maryland. At the time, the family still lived in northern Virginia, close to Washington, D.C., where her parents worked as freelance writers and co-hosted a show on public radio. They now lived in Boulder, Colorado, a bastion of aging "free spirits."

Their young, conservative daughter amused Norman and Marta and they smiled when she rebelliously dressed in plaid skirts, knee-high socks, leather loafers, white shirts and cardigan sweaters. They understood her need to "buck the establishment." The same need drove them into finding their destiny as teens, albeit with tied-dyed T-shirts and hemp sandals.

While her parents rambled, Sabrina grew up self-reliant and reserved. She spent most summers at Grandmother Rose's home in Eaton, Pennsylvania, while her parents rode elephants in India and Land Rovered through the Australian Outback. If anything, Norman and Marta were relieved that Sabrina wanted to attend a boarding school. It freed them of one more item on their checklist when traveling: Where to put Sabrina.

She sighed, pushing a weary hand through her dark, rumpled hair. "Alright; calm down. I'll go," she said.

"Good girl. I'll have Daddy text message you the details. Which hospital …"

"There's only one hospital in Eaton, Mom," Sabrina said, recalling the summer she broke her wrist. It prevented her from swimming at the community pool just when she learned how to dive. After the cast came off in August, her grandmother enrolled her in tennis lessons to build her wrist muscles. For the next few weeks, until she returned to Virginia for seventh grade, she swooned over Robert Hall, a pre-law college student who taught tennis at the rec center during summer vacations.

"Fine. Let me take care of a few things and I'll be there tomorrow."

"You mean tonight," her mother said.

Sabrina looked at her clock. The red digital numbers clicked to six a.m. and the alarm buzzed. Reaching out to slap the snooze button, she groaned. "Yes; I mean tonight. Good bye, Mom."

Sabrina worked from her apartment, the second floor of a 19th century row house remodeled into three levels of living. The landlord lived in the basement apartment, and an elderly married couple rented the first floor. The property owner's hobbies included gardening and he kept the small front yard blooming nearly year around. Instead of landscaping the backyard, he built small decks for each unit and filled them with potted trees, container gardens and patio furniture.

Renters appreciated the airy feel inside each apartment, thanks to the ivory walls and French doors opening onto the deck patio. Built-in oak shelving glowed, six-foot windows filled the rooms with light, and the kitchen was decorated in a Tuscany style. The effect was chic, yet homey, and the rent enormous, even for Baltimore.

Sabrina used her second bedroom as a home office where she operated her small financial consulting firm. Photographs from her parents adorned the walls. There were vistas of Mount Fuji, underwater shots of colorful fish and coral at the Great Barrier Reef, a photo of Norman and Marta in front of Stonehenge, and another of Marta racing the steps of a Mayan pyramid. There were no photos of Sabrina; she was never included in their journeys. Instead, they shuffled her to Grandmother Rose's home in Pennsylvania, or various college students would take turns house- and daughter-sitting for the Windhams.

She hated to leave her home, so after showering and packing a suitcase, Sabrina knocked with reluctance on the basement door.

"Mr. Brothers; it's me, Sabrina Windham," she called through the steel door, knowing from experience that he rose early.

Ricardo Brothers opened the door, a steaming mug of coffee in one hand.

"Good morning, Sabrina. What can I do for you?" His steady gaze dropped to the suitcase.

"I have to go to Pennsylvania for a while. I'm not sure how long. My grandmother is in the hospital," she said.

"Oh, I'm sorry to hear that." Ricardo took a sip of his coffee. The aroma of freshly ground Columbian beans filled the hallway.

"Would you please collect my mail and forward it to me? Here is the address," she said, handing him an envelope. "I've included some cash for postage. Also, will you take care of the plants? I watered them on Saturday, so they're good for a few more days."

"Certainly. Anything you need. You have my phone number and my e-mail, so please keep in touch. I hope your grandmother is better soon."

She nodded her thanks. A car honked.

"There's my taxi. I must run. Thank you, Mr. Brothers, I appreciate this."

Ricardo nodded, and then sipped his coffee as he watched Sabrina hurry up the concrete steps. His orange tabby cat wound through his ankles and meowed.

"Morning, Sally. Ready for your breakfast?" He closed the door and followed the cat into his tidy kitchen.

* * *

The small airplane dipped below the clouds then touched down. The tube shook and ill-fitting cabinet doors rattled as the wheels roared down the runway. It coasted to a stop and the seatbelt light snapped off. Sabrina waited for the other passengers to leave. She preferred to wait since the limited headroom on the "puddle jumper" plane meant she would have to crouch until others disembarked.

Across the aisle, a young mother cradled a sleeping infant over her shoulder. "You go ahead," she whispered as her harried husband struggled with the car seat.

Sabrina slid out of the cramped seat, opened the overhead storage and removed her briefcase. Packed with her notebook computer, cell phone, books and folders of pending work, the case weighed at least twenty pounds. She grunted, then shifted it in front of her, hoping it wouldn't throw her off balance as she exited the plane. She paused at the top of the folding stairs and looked around.

The small airport squatted in a valley, nestled between green mountains with fog-shrouded peaks. The Appalachians were old, their shoulders rounded from millions of years of wind and rain. Sabrina viewed this same scene for many summers, coming to and going from Grandmother Rose's house. Always, she made the trip alone.

The woman, who minutes earlier used orange-tipped flashlights to guide the turbo prop commuter, now drove an ATV with a trailer to the rear of the airplane. The steward opened the locker in the plane's belly and placed suitcases on the tarmac. The young woman, spry in a green, one-piece jumpsuit and yellow safety vest, slung the suitcases into the trailer.

"That it?"

The steward nodded and then tippled his fingers, miming a drink.

"Yeah, sure. I get off at four. See you at the pub?"

"I'll be there. I've got a couple of days off, so …"

Their voices lowered as they moved closer. The woman laughed and pushed at the young man's chest. "Perv!" She quickly kissed him and then sprang onto the seat of the tractor. "Gotta get these bags to the terminal. See you tonight."

Sabrina walked across the tarmac and entered the airport. In the lobby, people hugged and chatted with arriving passengers.

"Well, it's not much, but it has the right ingredients," Sabrina thought, glancing at the single security gate and the lone ticket window.

She headed for baggage claim, joining the other passengers in front of a set of garage doors. The metal dividers lifted noisily and Sabrina watched as the young woman from the ATV tossed the baggage onto a low-slung counter. She'd driven the tractor about fifty yards from the plane.

Sabrina found her bag, and then headed for the car rental counter when a short, elderly man stepped into her path.

"Excuse me, miss. Are you Sabrina Windham?"

Puzzled, she nodded. The man twisted a worn baseball cap in his hands. "I'm James Weaver; Rose's neighbor. The visiting nurse said you were coming in this afternoon and that I should offer you a ride."

"Thank you very much, Mr. Weaver," Sabrina said. "But, I'm going to need a car while I'm here in Eaton, so I'll rent one."

"Well, here's the thing. Miss Rose has a nice car and the nurse said you're to use that while you're here. It's a real nice one. Miss Rose always gets a new car every few years. It's right out front."

He shuffled towards a sliding glass door that parted when he passed its electric eye. Parked at the curb sat a Cadillac, its motor running and the radio tuned to a conservative talk show.

Sabrina smiled at the small-town charm that allowed people to leave cars running when performing brief chores. Locked doors in Eaton are rare.

James pushed the key fob and the trunk popped opened. He took her suitcase and hefted it into the voluminous trunk, then slammed the lid. Scooting to the passenger door, he opened it, gallantly standing to the side.

"Thank you," Sabrina said, sliding into the elegant, full-size automobile that flouted her parent's ideology of hybrid fuels and conservation. She caressed the leather interior. I am, she thought, my grandmother's daughter.

In only fifteen minutes, her plane landed, she claimed her luggage and was on the road. Small towns have their rewards and a lack of traffic and tiny airports are the best, she reflected.

"Have you ever been to Eaton?" James tried to restart the car, the ignition system grinding. He grimaced. "Oops. Forgot it was already on." He slipped the gearshift into drive and without looking over his shoulder, made a quick U-turn and drove out of the airport parking lot.

"Yes," Sabrina said. "My parents traveled a lot, so I spent most of my summers here with Grandmother Rose."

The old man nodded, not paying attention to her chatty reply. He drove along River Road toward Eaton. "River's up," he commented.

Sabrina glanced at the water, its ripples glinting in the late afternoon sun. "Has it been a wet summer?"

He nodded, then spent the next few minutes recounting the increasing number of storms. "One good thing about the rain," he added, "is the fall leaves will be grand. That should bring more visitors."

He turned into a quiet neighborhood lined with Victorian mansions and spreading maple trees. Some houses were modified into apartments for college students, others into offices for lawyers and doctors.

The local preservation foundation owned a few historic houses, selling them to wealthy residents who could afford the restoration and the upkeep. Most were included on the foundation's annual Victorian homes tour. Rose owned such a house, with each rose-themed room decorated in a different color. Sabrina stayed in the yellow "Lord Mountbatten Rose" room when she visited.

Sabrina studied the elderly man as he drove. He seemed to be in his mid-seventies, possibly eighties, but appeared strong. She wondered who he was and how he knew her grandmother. She didn't know James Weaver, although she hadn't been to visit for a few years.

"Do you know anything about her accident?"

He glanced at Sabrina apologetically. "Not much. She was alone. Doctors say she had a stroke. She was on the floor all night until my wife stopped by the next morning. She saw her at the bottom of the staircase. 'Bout had a heart attack, herself. She thought the poor old woman fell down the steps and killed herself. Doctor thinks she was sitting on the bottom step, trying to catch her breath when she keeled over."

Sabrina's eyes filled with tears. Grandmother Rose had always been kind to her, although Sabrina could well imagine her as the evil stepmother in a cartoon. She was tall, rail thin with silver hair swept into a chignon. She always wore haute couture, even though she rarely left her house.

To Sabrina, Grandmother Rose seemed a haunted woman who denied herself the pleasure and love of people, but not the pleasure of things. She seemed to enjoy her oriental vases and bronze statues more than her own son and his family.

As a beautiful and wealthy young widow, Rose Windham should have been the belle of the ball. Instead, after she moved to Eaton in 1976, the town's residents learned that the haughty woman didn't want friends.

Sabrina knew that her father felt slighted by Rose. She shuttled him off to prep school the year his father died, and then sent him to a military academy for college. In his junior year, he withdrew, making a list of the top ten liberal colleges in the nation and applying to all.

He chose Hampshire College in Amherst, Massachusetts, for its particularly open-minded reputation. There, he reveled in socially conscious, left-wing repartee and indulged in artistic expression, majoring in theater with a minor in psychology.

At Hampshire, he met the love of his life, Marta, a beautiful Brazilian exchange student majoring in creative writing. Throughout their bohemian life, they managed to rear their daughter, Sabrina, in turn, rebelled against her parents and sought education at a private girls' prep school. She followed that with Harvard's business school and studied finance.

She blinked back her tears as James pulled into the alley behind the mansion, parking the car in the carriage house.

"We're here."

"We're not going to the hospital?"

"She refused to stay. She's been released and has a nurse to take care of her at home."

Nothing could have prepared Sabrina for the sight of the fragile, pale woman. Rose's body barely mounded the quilts of the hospital bed, incongruous in the dining room.

The crystal chandelier above Rose's head cast a yellow and ghastly light. Her nose, once aristocratic, now seemed hawkish, her mouth encircled with deep lines. Glazed blue eyes pinned hers when Sabrina walked to the bed and gently picked up the bone-thin hand.

"Grandmother?"

"Sabrina," the elderly woman whispered, a tear rolling down the tissue-thin cheek.

"I'm here, Grandmother."

"Norman?" The old woman's eyes darted behind Sabrina, falling upon her neighbor, James.

"He couldn't come, Grandmother. They're in Tibet," she lied.

Rose Windham closed her eyes and sighed. A moment later, her fingers tightened. "Thank you, darling girl."

Sabrina sat by Rose's bed for several silent minutes, watching as the woman fell asleep. Then, she went looking for answers.

She found the nurse in the kitchen. The steaming teakettle stopped whistling as the young woman lifted it from the flame. She looked up briefly, nodded at Sabrina, and then concentrated on filling her teacup with the boiling water.

"Hello. You must be Miss Windham," she said, setting the kettle back on the stove. After wiping her hands on her blue hospital scrubs, she extended one to Sabrina. "I'm Shirley Piper. I'm an R.N., and I'll be taking care of your grandmother."

Sabrina nodded, pleased by the woman's confidence. "Call me Sabrina, please. It's nice to meet you."

"And call me Shirley. You'll want an update on your grandmother, but can I fix you a cup of tea first?"

Sabrina recognized fragrant chamomile and grimaced. After drinking herbal tea all her childhood, she forswore it as an adult.

"Thanks, but I'll pass. I've got bottled water in my bag."

Shirley nodded and leaned against the counter. She lifted the cup to her lips and blew.

"Your grandmother fell, injuring her pelvis. Or, at her age, her pelvis may have fractured first, causing the fall."

"Excuse me? How does that happen?"

"Your grandmother has severe osteoporosis, also called brittle bone syndrome by some people. It is a wasting away of the bone that happens as women age. Bone breaks down more quickly than it is replaced, so bones weaken and may fracture. There are medications that prevent or treat osteoporosis, but she has not been taking them.

"She also suffered a transient ischemic attack. You may have heard them called mini-strokes. These occur when the supply of oxygen is cut off to an area of the brain. Unlike a stroke, which is often permanent, the symptoms of a transient ischemic attack last less than a day, usually less than ten minutes."

Sabrina took a deep breath. It was the first piece of good news she'd heard today.

Shirley sipped her tea again. "The problem is that anyone who has a transient ischemic attack is at risk of developing a stroke in the future. Your grandmother is at risk, and a major stroke can be crippling, or even cause death."

"What can we do?"

"She refuses to stay at the hospital, and since she has plenty of money and her doctor under her thumb, she's insisted that we take care of her here. The problem with that is the limited amount of medical equipment available. We have established a hospital-room setting here, with oxygen and a heart monitor. I've started an I.V. to make sure she has her liquids. She's also on a blood thinner. We have contractors coming in tomorrow to modify the downstairs bathroom, to make it more accessible."

"Do you think she should be in the hospital? Do you want me to try to talk her into going back?"

"You can try if you like, but I've known Miss Rose for a few years, and I've never met a more stubborn, hard-headed woman. You see, my daddy is Dr. Piper, the physician under her thumb." Shirley gently added, "You need to understand that Miss Rose is getting old, and she is a frail woman. We can take care of her to a certain degree, but her biggest battle is time and nobody wins that one."

Sabrina nodded. "I understand, and you're right. It's important to make her comfortable. Is this a hospice situation? Is Grandmother Rose dying?"

"No, nothing like that. She can recover from this and live many more years. On the other hand, she could suffer more TIAs until she has a major stroke. There are no guarantees. She knows that. That's why she wants to be home. I suggest you make the most of the time that's left. Do you plan to stay awhile?"

"I really don't know. I haven't made any plans. I found

out this morning that she was ill, so I hopped the next available flight out of Baltimore."

"Well, I can take care of her body. Only you can help her soul. Seems to me, that's what's been causing her the most pain."

Sabrina thanked the young nurse, wise beyond her years. She returned to her grandmother's bedside and, for the next hour, held her hand, comforting the old woman.

At midnight, Shirley Piper went off duty and another nurse, an older woman with beefy arms and a kind face, began the late shift. Rose would have around-the-clock care.

Sabrina stood and stretched. She looked for her suitcase and briefcase, and found them by the front door where she dropped them. Exhausted, she dragged them upstairs to her yellow rose room. Too tired to undress, she kicked her shoes off and climbed under the covers. Within moments, she was asleep.

CHAPTER TWO

For the next few days, Sabrina visited quietly with her grandmother. She gave the nurses the space and privacy they needed as they developed a routine for caring for the elderly woman. Rose slept for hours, thanks to the scheduled morphine shots to ease her pain. Sabrina filled her free time wandering around the mansion, organizing books on shelves, dusting knickknacks, and rearranging photographs of Norman and Marta in foreign locales.

Ricardo Brothers began forwarding her mail, and she arranged an alcove in the sitting room as her new office. The kindly landlord also adopted her houseplants, keeping them on his patio until her return. She had few clients since her business was new, and for one-on-one consultations, she referred them to a reliable financial pro. She hoped they would reconsider her services when she returned.

One afternoon, bored and snooping, she discovered a scrapbook and a collection of letters and journals tucked in the antique chest in her grandmother's dressing room.

Sabrina felt guilty as she untied the lilac ribbon that encircled the letters. She seldom ventured into her grandmother's bedroom as a child, intimidated by the lavender gloom and the overwhelming scent of roses. It reminded her of a mausoleum.

This afternoon, however, she pulled the long, heavy drapes away from the window, turned on the bedside lamps and spread the items on the satin coverlet. Some of the letters were in her grandmother's handwriting. Others were from Don Windham, Rose's late husband. There were some letters with no return name on the envelope. Sabrina didn't know where to start, and her stomach flip-flopped.

I'm not meddling. I'm researching family history, she told herself.

She sorted the letters according to the dates on the postmarks. They ranged from 1955 to 1975, twenty years of Rose's life. She also organized the journals, starting with the earliest. They began in 1965, and ended in 1975.

"As if she stopped living when Grandfather died," Sabrina murmured. "Why? What happened?"

Sabrina never knew her family's history. Norman preferred to live in the present, never mentioning his father, never talking about his own childhood. Marta talked about her childhood, but it was a bittersweet story of a young Brazilian orphan brought up by affectionate Catholic nuns. Born Marta Valente, she did not know her mother or father, and had no family until she met Norman in college. It was an important connection: Both felt abandoned, alone, until they found each other. The difference was, Norman did have Rose, a wealthy, yet distant, mother.

When Sabrina was born, the thrilled couple had no idea how to form a family. Instead, they viewed Sabrina as a toy, almost a pet.

Impatient, Sabrina picked up the last letter, dated December 12, 1975. It was a small, creased envelope with no return address. With shaky fingers, Sabrina extracted the one-page note. The edges were torn, the blue ink faded and, in some parts, stained. Tears?

"I must see you again. It can't end this way. Meet me tonight. Believe me, Rose. We can do this. We deserve this. D."

Sabrina frowned, then re-read the letter.

"D?" Don Windham? Was she planning to leave him? Had she already left him and he wanted her back?

She picked up another letter, this one a brief note from Don Windham.

"Rose, Delivered the boat. It handled well, even in Force 8 winds off Bar Harbor. Be home soon. Love, Don."

Sabrina glanced at the postmark on the envelope: September 21, 1975. She picked up the first letter and held one in each hand, comparing the script. They were dissimilar. Even the paper and the envelopes were distinct, although that wouldn't make much difference.

The style of writing and the context were different. One was passionate and pleading, the other, matter-of-fact and upbeat. Two men: A lover and a husband, and she lost both sometime in 1975, because Sabrina knew that Rose moved to Eaton, alone, in 1976. Norman, enrolled in a prep school in Virginia, seldom came home.

She opened several more letters, three from the mysterious "D" and two from Don Windham, dating from 1974 to 1975. Again, "D" wrote short love letters begging her to meet him, while Don Windham wrote of various business contacts he made while traveling throughout New England, including boat orders, and sea conditions.

Sabrina didn't bother reading any of the other, older letters. Instead, she picked up the latest journal and tabbed through the pages to the final entry.

"December 10, 1975. Christmas shopping today. I'm in New York at the Plaza, loving every moment. Macy's is fantastic and I had the best time at FAO Schwarz. I picked up a Pong game for Norman, some

kind of video game that connects to the television. Now that he's fifteen, he doesn't want to play with his action figures anymore. I also found a pretty cashmere sweater for Margaret. Don wouldn't come. Said he had work to do and couldn't afford the time. He infuriates me. He certainly can afford the time; he just will not do it. He refuses to use any of daddy's money, as usual. Obstinate man. We could be living in a beautiful home instead of a hovel. I'm so tired of doing without, when we have my inheritance just sitting in the bank. He won't let me invest a dime in the business, saying its 'the man's job to take care of the family.' At least he couldn't stop me from sending Norman to school. It felt so good to spend money today without Don asking to see my checkbook. I'm glad he didn't come with me. I'm going to take a long bubble bath, and I've ordered champagne and dinner for two. I damn well intend to enjoy my last night in New York. D will be here soon. I'm sure he'll appreciate my shopping today."

Sabrina flipped through the journal, checking entries for the initial "D," and finding it on nearly every page.

"Grandmother Rose! I can't believe what I'm reading," she said, biting her lip.

Sabrina picked up the scrapbook and slowly turned the pages filled with newspaper clippings, postcards and photographs; each carefully taped or anchored with black corners. This book also stopped in 1975.

It's as if she died, too, Sabrina thought. Then, she found a folded newspaper article, shoved between the last two pages. She read the headline and gasped.

"Boat Builder, Partner Killed in Midnight Blaze, Factory Destroyed in Three-Alarm Fire."

There was no date at the top of the clipping. She read the rest of the article.

"NEWPORT – Boat builder Donald N. Windham, 45, and his partner, Derek F. West, 44, died Friday in a midnight blaze that destroyed the Zephyrus Boatyard and injured one person, Rose Windham, 35.

Three fire companies and the local police responded to the tragedy, which is still being investigated. Fire Chief Flip Jenkins reported that the inferno started in an office, perhaps by a faulty kerosene stove, and spread throughout the shop quickly. Fifty-gallon barrels of resin and stacks of plywood, used in the manufacturing of fiberglass boats, were "like jet fuel on the fire. The Jakes (fire fighters) couldn't get close enough to put it out," Jenkins said.

Fire fighters were forced to battle not only searing flames and choking black smoke but also a lack of water. Jenkins said that there were no fire hydrants nearby, and the plant's water supply was inadequate for fighting such a massive fire. The roof and all but one wall of the two-story metal building collapsed, forcing fire fighters to flee the structure.

Rose Windham was treated for smoke inhalation and second-degree burns at the scene. Police responding to the fire said she will be questioned later and that, at this point, she is the only eye-witness to the tragedy."

Sabrina stared, open-mouthed, at the newspaper article. She assumed that Don Windham had died of natural causes. No one volunteered details and she never asked about her family's history.

Her hands shook and she wanted to call her father, but he and Marta were already in Tibet, wandering about on the backs of ponies.

How much does he know? He must know all, Sabrina reasoned. But why hadn't he ever told her?

That evening, Sabrina sat quietly at her grandmother's bedside. Together, they watched the news and then the cable's travel channel with Rose hoping for a glimpse of her famous son. His and Marta's documentaries were popular reruns.

Sabina adjusted the bed at a slight incline, enabling Rose to view the large, flat-panel television the contractors installed on the dining room wall. Sabrina wondered how long the 150-year-old plaster walls would support the heavy screen.

The nurse placed a nightstand with a portable telephone and a pitcher of violet-scented water next to the hospital bed, and plumped satin cushions behind Rose's back. Morphine and glucose water dripped steadily into the back of the old woman's blue-veined hand.

A hairdresser had washed and styled Rose's hair. Wearing a frilly lavender nightgown, her silver hair combed into its smooth chignon, she appeared to be on the mend.

"Grandmother," Sabrina said, then cleared her throat. "May I speak to you about something personal?"

Rose flinched, then closed her eyes. "Of course you can."

"Do you miss my grandfather? Do you miss Don Windham?"

Rose's chest heaved slightly, a deep sigh emanated from the small, shrunken woman.

"Every day."

"Did you love him?"

"Of course I did. I love Norman and you, too. Is that what you want to know?"

"No, Grandmother. I know you love me," Sabrina said, reaching out and stroking Rose's quilted leg. "I know you love Daddy, too. It's just that you never talk about my grandfather, and I'd like to know about him. I'd like to know what your life was like when you were a young woman."

"I see." Rose paused, licking her thin, pale lips. "Well, I'm not sure where to begin. It's been such a long time."

"Why don't you tell me how you met?"

"Please, would you hand me a glass of water?"

Sabrina complied, and Rose sipped, her forehead puckering thoughtfully.

"Well, I was very young, barely seventeen when I first saw Don. He was ten years older than me, and working at a boatyard in Rhode Island. That's where he was born. That's where Norman was born."

Sabrina nodded, but said nothing.

"My family lived in New York City and spent summers on Long Island, in the Hamptons."

Sabrina waited. Rose closed her eyes as if seeing her childhood home again.

"Daddy ordered a new sailboat and a handsome young skipper delivered it from Rhode Island. Daddy asked me to handle the jib, and the three of us sailed all afternoon. Don Windham was so serious and capable. I still remember how his hair curled and whipped in the breeze. He was supposed to return to Rhode Island by ferry, but we kept him on the water so long, that he missed the last one. Daddy invited him to stay for dinner and the night. He slept on the boat."

Rose sipped her water.

"That night, I went to him and we talked for hours under the stars. We sat in the cockpit until dawn. When he kissed me goodbye, I knew I had to have him.

"Of course, Daddy was not happy about that. He had other plans for me. He wanted me to marry the son of his banker. A moron. I told him I wanted to marry Don. We wrote to each other. He would come to New York on the train and I'd meet him at a hotel. This went on for about a year, then Don said I needed to make a choice. Either I stand up to Daddy and marry him, or else."

"Or else, what?" Sabrina asked when Rose paused.

"I didn't want to know what else," she said. "I was eighteen and could legally marry, so we went to the justice of the peace that afternoon. We told Mother, and she called Daddy. He never forgave me, and he refused to come home if Don was there."

"What did you do?"

"I packed a couple of suitcases and caught the train to Rhode Island with Don. We lived in a small cottage by the bay while he worked at one boatyard after another until he could open his own. I didn't see Daddy for two years, not until after Norman was born.

"Then, when Norman was five, my father died and I received my inheritance. We were suddenly rich. But Don wouldn't take any of the money. He wouldn't use it to build the business. You see, my father said terrible things to me after the wedding. He broke my heart and Don never forgave him.

"I forgave him. I would take baby Norman home to New York and visit my parents. We would go shopping or skating in the winter, and in the summer, we sailed around Long Island and played on the beach. It was almost like being a girl again, this time with Norman as a little playmate. But Don was never with us."

"How sad."

"I thought so, at first. Then I became angry. Don was stubborn and proud, even after my father died. He resented the man when he was alive, and more so when he was dead. He once told me he wished that I'd never inherited the money, that it only cursed our family."

"How did it curse the family?"

Rose glanced at Sabrina, then frowned. "What? Oh, I'm sorry, dear. I've been rambling. I'm very tired now. Would you turn out the light?"

Rose's recollections had been clear and she seemed eager to share. Sabrina speculated about the abrupt dismissal, but didn't want to upset her.

"Sure, Grandmother." Sabrina reached for the lamp

and tugged on the cord. She picked up the remote control and placed it on Rose's lap. "Here; just in case you want to watch TV for a while. Goodnight," she said, and kissed her grandmother's cheek.

Rose placed a trembling hand on Sabrina's face. "Goodnight." She closed her eyes.

Two days passed and Sabrina wanted to speak with Rose again. She read all the letters, read the journals, and finished the scrapbook. She had a suspicion that the mysterious "D" was Derek West, but she wanted Rose to confirm it.

More than that, for the first time in her life she felt a family connection, a legacy. During the night, as she turned past events over in her mind, a plan evolved. Excited, she wanted Rose to approve of her idea.

She couldn't wait to get started, but she dreaded telling Rose that she pried into her personal letters.

Hoping that breakfast would pave the way, she carried a tray with two cups of coffee and toasted English muffins into the dining room.

"Good morning, Grandmother," she said, smiling. She placed the tray on the nightstand and picked up her coffee mug. "Mmmmm, this smells good."

Rose picked up her dainty, rose-embellished cup. She sipped, then placed it back on the tray. "Thank you, dear. Muffins? You have more faith in my teeth than I do." She tore off a corner and popped it in her mouth.

"I want to talk to you about something. Something I think is important."

"What is it, dear?" Rose asked.

"First, I have something to confess, and second, I have a plan I'd like to discuss. I've done something inexcusable, and you need to know. You also need to understand that I'm not sorry for what I've done; I'm only sorry that it may hurt you."

"Oh my goodness, what have you done?" Rose, thoroughly alarmed now, struggled to sit up.

Sabrina placed a restraining hand on her tiny shoulder. "No; don't get up. I found your journals and your letters. I've read them."

Rose collapsed onto the soft pillows, her eyes confused. "My letters?"

Sabrina nodded.

Rose's mouthed twisted, her eyes darted back and forth, then rested on Sabrina. "You mean you've only now found them? You never were a nosy child, were you?"

It was Sabrina's turn to gawk. "You mean, you don't mind?"

Rose laughed gently. "I'm on my deathbed. Well, it could be my deathbed. My secrets have haunted me all my life. Do you think I want to take them to my grave?"

Sabrina leaned closer to the bed. "Tell me about my grandfather. Then tell me about the fire. Tell me about Derek West and his family. Why did you move here to Eaton?"

Rose sighed. "Well, that's going to take a while. I told you about my father, and how Don stubbornly refused to speak with him. This went on for many years, and after my father died, Don still refused to acknowledge or visit my mother.

"I was lonely and angry and wanted to punish him. Derek and Don were childhood friends, closer than brothers were. I wanted to hurt Don, so I came between them. It was ...." Rose paused and wiped a tear. "It was a tragic decision. I killed the man I loved, and I killed his best friend. I can never forgive myself for that."

With this, Rose bowed her head and tears fell silently into her lap.

"Grandmother! What are you saying?" Sabrina sat back in the chair, thunderstruck.

"You read the newspaper clipping about the fire? Why do you think they died and I didn't? Don followed me that night and they fought. I got between them but they pushed me away. I must have fallen and hit my head. I blacked out and, to this day, I don't know how the fire started. The police said a kerosene stove had been knocked over. The next thing I knew, I was in the boatyard and the building was on fire. I saw Don running back in, calling to Derek. Then, the roof collapsed and I never saw either of them alive again.

"It's so strange to tell it aloud. For thirty-five years, I've replayed the scene in my head. Not a day goes by that I don't think about Don, and about Derek, and how my foolish, selfish heart killed them both. How could I forgive myself?"

Sabrina let out a deep breath. "My God, Grandmother. All these years, the burden you've been carrying."

"It's mine, child. I've none to blame but myself."

"It was an accident, Grandmother. You didn't start the fire."

"If I hadn't been unfaithful, if I hadn't been with Derek that night, they wouldn't have fought and the fire wouldn't have started. They would not have died. Those are the facts, Sabrina."

"Does my father know?"

"I'm sure he does. He was fifteen then, almost a young man. He read the papers. He knew Derek's family. At the funeral, Faye West, Derek's wife, was hysterical, screaming that it was my fault, that I was a whore and a murderer. I suppose that Norman figured something was wrong when I grabbed his hand and we ran for the car. I never returned. I kept driving until we reached New York. Soon, I bought this house and moved to Eaton. Norman returned to school. We never spoke about it."

Sabrina rocked back and forth in her chair, her arms crossed over her chest.

"It must have been a nightmare for you."

"It still is."

That evening, Rose suffered another mini stroke and was rushed to the emergency room. Sabrina paced the hospital hall, biting her lip and brushing away tears.

At the sight of Shirley Piper, she nearly collapsed.

"How is she? Is she going to be alright?"

"It's not a serious episode, but like I told you, these TIAs are leading to a major stroke."

"It's my fault," Sabrina wailed, her hands shoved into her jean's pockets.

"Don't be ridiculous," Shirley said. "Your grandmother has enjoyed being with you. I've never seen her so happy."

"No, I mean today, I ... she ... we were talking about my grandfather and it brought up bad memories. I should never have spoken to her about him."

Shirley patted Sabrina's arm. "Honey; you're here to be with your grandmother through the good and the bad. You both need this time. You're not to blame for the tiny blood clots that move through her brain. Those are the cause of her strokes, not talking to you about the past. Why don't you go in and see her? She's awake and asking for you."

"Thanks, Shirley."

With a deep breath, Sabrina opened the hospital door. Blue-tinged neon light bathed Grandmother Rose. The clear vinyl tube attached to her nose hissed as it fed oxygen into her bloodstream.

Rose's eyes opened and she rested her dreamy gaze on Sabrina.

"Hello. I suppose it happened again?"

"Yes. I'm worried about you. I'm so sorry. I should never have brought up the past."

"Nonsense. It's never far from my mind. I am relieved that you know. You're my confessor now."

"Grandmother, I don't want to hurt you."

"You can't, Sabrina. By the way, you never told me your plan."

She cringed. "It's nothing, really."

"Tell me. I need the diversion."

Sabrina squirmed. "I don't think it's a good idea. I've already changed my mind, anyway."

Rose sighed. "Tell me."

"All right. I was thinking about finding Grandfather's first boat, if it still exists, and buying it. I think, if I have something he created, I could feel a connection. I haven't touched the trust fund you gave me when I turned twenty-five."

Rose's eyes flew open. "Goodness gracious!"

"I told you it was a bad idea."

"Indeed, I think it's a wonderful idea. I've often wondered what happened to all those boats. They were quite popular, although the run was short. Your grandfather was a genius, and his boats were beautiful."

"Then you don't mind?"

"Not at all. I wish I'd thought of it."

Tremulous, Sabrina smiled. "Thank you, Grandmother."

CHAPTER THREE

The gaff-rigged sail of the graceful catboat filled as it slid from its mooring on the Warren River in Rhode Island. The young boy tacked back and forth in five-knot winds.

On the shore, the boy's father watched. "She's beautiful, Jay. Just like the day my daddy bought her for me," he said, emotion making his voice crack. "Brady's been pestering me for a boat of his own, and I'm glad you talked me into restoring her instead of buying a new dinghy."

Humbled, Jay West shoved his hands in his jeans pockets. "You're welcome, Sam. We enjoyed working on a classic Marshall, and the Sandpiper is a nice little boat."

Pride warred with worry in the mother's eyes. "You don't think it's too much for him, do you?" she asked Jay. "Are you sure he can handle it?"

"Catboats are very stable thanks to their wide beam, Melinda. He'll do fine in these winds, but I wouldn't let him go out in anything above ten knots. At least, not until he's a bit more experienced. Swimming is a great teacher. Just make sure he wears a life jacket and stays on the river," he said.

"I can't wait to sail her," Sam enthused. "Thanks again," he said, shaking Jay's hand.

"You're welcome." Jay looked at his watch. "Well, I have to lock up now. He's sailing it home, right? You want us to deliver the trailer?"

"Yes; that'd be great. We're going to keep it at the dock for the summer, so just leave the trailer by the garage."

"Right; I'll have Brett drop it off later. See you, folks," he said.

Walking back to the boatyard, Jay whistled under his breath. Sam was a good customer. As commodore of the local yacht club, he often referred Jay's boatyard to its membership.

In the two years that he and Brett Story operated the Warren Boatyard, they kept busy, but busy wasn't enough. The yacht club had plenty of members and many aging sailboats, but they wanted the big, dramatic restoration jobs. The jobs that brought national attention and mentions in popular sailing magazines.

Brett looked up from the rope he'd been splicing. "How'd it go?"

"Perfect. Thanks for giving their son lessons last week. You should have seen their faces. I swear, they almost cried watching him sail off into the sunset."

"Makes it worthwhile, doesn't it?"

Jay patted the folded check in his T-shirt pocket. "That and four grand."

* * *

A weekend spent searching the Internet gave Sabrina's spirit a boost. It turned out that the Zephyrus was now considered a "Classic Plastic," and enjoyed a cult following. She learned that Classic Plastic is another way of saying a well-built fiberglass boat, and the West Wind-designed Zephyrus had timeless appeal. She found several photographs of the double-ended daysailer, each identified by hull number. An advanced search yielded nothing about Hull Number One, her quest.

She drove downtown to Sullivan's, the local bookshop, but found in its place a new store named East of Eaton. She snickered at the shop's name, a play on words and homage to John Steinbeck's classic novel "East of Eden."

She pushed open the heavy oak door and entered a bibliophile's wonderland. Her eyes widened at the view that included rows upon rows of new bookcases. A staircase wound its way up to a cafe. The aroma of fresh ground coffee beans and chocolate chip cookies assaulted her senses. As she let the door close, she glimpsed a customer behind her. Too late, she extended her arm to hold the door and instead struck the man in the shoulder.

"Oh, excuse me," she murmured, then froze at the sight of her girlhood crush.

Robert Hall glanced at her with impatience, then paused. "Sabrina?" he asked. "What brings you to Eaton?"

She flushed and fumbled with an apology. "Oh, so sorry. Robert Hall? It's been years since I've last seen you. Rose had a stroke and she's in the hospital. I'm here to take of her."

"I'm sorry to hear that," Robert said, stepping aside to allow yet another customer in the store. "Will she be alright?"

Sabrina chewed her bottom lip and twisted her head to hide eyes bright with unshed tears. Robert watched as she shrugged, the simple gesture was heart wrenching.

"Let's step over here," he said, his hand light on her elbow. He led her to a quiet area of the shop, shielding her from curious customers' view with his broad shoulders.

Not wanting to speak about Rose, knowing she would lose control and cry, she lifted her chin and asked, "How are you, Robert? Did you finish law school?"

He recalled the gangly girl from his summer job at the local rec center. "Yes. Do you still play tennis?"

Sabrina rolled her eyes and shook her head. "No, sorry.

Your lessons were wasted on me."

"Where do you live now?" he asked, his appreciation growing for the exotic, beautiful woman.

"I have an apartment in Baltimore where I run a small financial business," she said, pausing when Robert looked over his shoulder at the woman at the front counter. He nodded once, as if in silent agreement with her.

Sabrina assessed the woman, noting her delicate beauty even from half across the store. Unruly, dark brown hair crowned her oval face; dark brown eyes watched her curiously.

"Is she your girlfriend?" Sabrina asked, inclining her head.

Robert flashed a grin. "No, that's Erica Moore. We're business partners."

"So you're part owner of this bookstore?" Sabrina asked, surveying the elegant yet practical furnishings. "Why am I not surprised?"

He looked at his watch, already withdrawing. "I have to meet with a client in a few minutes, but I'd like to see you again. Would you have dinner with me while you're in town? Say, Friday?"

Was Robert Hall asking her on a date? Her lips parted as her breath hitched. "It depends upon Rose. How she's doing by then. Why don't I give you a call later this week?"

Robert pulled a small silver case out of the inner pocket of his expensive suit coat and withdrew a business card. Using a slim Cross fountain pen, he scratched a note on the embossed card. "Here's my cell phone number if you can't reach me at the office," he said, holding out the card.

As Sabrina reached for it, he cupped her hands. Leaning forward, he brushed a soft kiss upon her cheek. "I am sorry Rose is ill."

A bit stunned by his closeness and sudden attention, Sabrina could only lift her head and nod. He squeezed her hands gently, then let her go. Whether it was small-town friendliness or something more, Sabrina's knees nearly buckled. She tucked the business card into her back pocket, then walked away, covertly watching as Robert approached the woman at the counter. They spoke for a minute or two, then he patted the woman's hand. Once again, he reached into his suit pocket and this time extracted some folded documents. He placed them on the counter then left the shop, but not before glancing across the stacks at Sabrina. She flushed as he caught her eye. Busted, she thought. Pretending she hadn't been gawking, she lifted her hand in a gesture of farewell.

Frozen with indecision, Sabrina looked at the bookcase in front of her. Why was she here? What was it she wanted? A few moments later, the shop owner ambled over and extended a hand in greeting.

"Welcome to East of Eaton. Are you looking for anything in particular?"

Sabrina blinked to clear her vision. "I'm looking for books on sailboats."

Erica pointed towards the back wall. "There's not a lot on that topic since we're a mountain town, but I do have a few. They're in the sports and recreation section."

Sabrina thanked her and wandered in the opposite direction. Eventually, she made her way to the back of the shop and perused the titles. There were a couple of illustrated books on tying knots, another book on trailer sailing, and yet another on fixing old boats. She picked up the ubiquitous yellow-and-black, how-to manual for "dummies" and leafed through the pages. She opted for the handyman book and the how-to manual, then browsed her way to the popular paperback novels. She pulled a couple bestsellers off the shelves, piled them on her growing stack of books and headed for the cash register.

This time, a petite elder woman worked behind the cash register. Her name tag identified her as "June Duval." She beamed at Sabrina as she placed the books on the counter. The shop owner wandered over while June rang up the sale.

"I see you found a few books," Erica said, glancing at the titles.

Sabrina nodded. "Yes, thanks. You're right, there's not much on sailing but I did find a couple novels since I'll be in town for a while."

"Robert tells me your grandmother is Rose Windham. I hear she's in the hospital. I hope it's not serious."

Sabrina frowned, her eyes bright again with unshed tears. "I hope so too," she whispered. She nodded her thanks, accepted the paper bag of books and quickly exited the shop.

On the drive home, she thought about the crushingly handsome Robert Hall. She felt a thrill of excitement at the idea of dinner with him. Did he know of her schoolgirl crush? Would he be flattered or feel harassed?

* * *

Several days passed without any clues on the lost Zephyrus sailboat. She created accounts for all the major Internet sailing forums and read comment threads. She placed classified ads in several New England newspapers and even hired a private investigator, hoping he could find some records, any that hadn't been destroyed in the fire.

Rose, who agreed to stay in the hospital temporarily, monitored her granddaughter's search. "You should look in the attic. I kept several boxes of Don's paperwork that he stored at home. Maybe you can find an old invoice."

Sabrina needed the breakthrough. She located the boxes and after opening one, inhaled the aroma of cherry tobacco, Old Spice and paper. She recognized the carved mahogany pipe that her grandfather clenched between his teeth in every old photograph. She pressed a handkerchief to her cheek, reveling in the cologne that still clung to the linen fabric.

She created piles, sorting the papers into stacks of invoices, receipts, lists and business correspondence. The earliest invoice for the selling price of a Zephyrus, $5,000, was dated March 1969, paid in full by someone named Blair.

It's a start, she thought, and tucked the invoice into her pocket. Later, again on the Internet, she searched the online telephone directory for any Blairs living in Rhode Island. She quickly narrowed her search to those living along the coast. She assumed that anyone with a boat needed a place to put it.

She found forty listings and printed the list.

She started with the Blairs (she assumed it would be a man) who lived closest to Warren, where the Zephyrus had been built. On her seventh call, she reached an elderly man. Having polished her speech, Sabrina launched into a quick introduction.

"Hello, my name is Sabrina Windham. My grandfather, Don Windham, designed the Zephyrus sailboat. I'm trying to locate a Mr. Blair who may have purchased one. Do you know anything about this boat?"

She paused. After a second or two, the querulous voice responded. "Sailboat? Eh? You looking for Don Windham's sailboat?"

Finally, a lead in her quest. Sabrina's heart raced. "Yes, do you know anything about a Zephyrus sailboat?"

"Sailboat, eh? Yes, I have one. It's in sorry shape, girly. You don't want this one."

Excited, Sabrina paced the sitting room ignoring his comment about the boat's condition. "You have a Zephyrus? May I ask you, which year?"

"Eh? Speak up, girly. I don't hear so well."

"Sorry," she raised her voice. "What year was the boat built?"

"Why, the first year, girly. Don Windham owed me money for a truck and trailer, so he traded me a new boat for it."

Sabrina pumped her fist excitedly.

"Mr. Blair, I would like to visit you and look at this

boat. Is that okay? Will you allow me to see it?"

"Sure; I don't mind. She's been sitting by the barn for nearly twenty years now. Put 'er in storage after I retired. Kids didn't want it, and I'm too old to sail a fast boat."

Sabrina confirmed his address and told him she would be in Rhode Island on Saturday. Again, using the Internet, she made a hotel reservation near Mr. Blair's zip code. Then she hurried to the hospital to update Rose.

"I don't know, Grandmother. This could be it," she said, her cheeks flushed.

Rose raised a weak hand, which Sabrina grasped.

"I hope so, dear. Mr. Blair? I don't remember him, but I do remember Don coming home one night with a dreadful truck and trailer. The thing was a rust bucket. It had a dragging muffler and it backfired when he revved the engine."

Rose closed her eyes and smiled, as if reliving the joy of an argument with her long-gone husband. "Don had just started building boats, and he said he needed a truck to move them to the dock. I don't remember if he traded the first one they built."

"I'm going to see Mr. Blair this weekend. He lives near Warren, Rhode Island. That's where you and Grandfather lived, isn't it?"

Rose nodded. "Yes. It's a small town on the Warren River, north of Narragansett Bay. Not many people lived there, but it was close to Providence, as well as Newport and Bristol. And, we could afford the rent."

"May I use your car, Grandmother?"

"Certainly, dear. I'm not going anywhere."

Friday approached and Sabrina decided to keep her dinner date with Robert Hall. She felt a bit guilty, going out while Rose lay in the hospital, but the old woman insisted.

"I don't want you rattling around in that old, drafty

house every night," Rose cautioned.

Sabrina acquiesced, but pointed out the obvious. "You rattle around in it and have for decades."

"That's different. I'm an old woman and I deserve to live with my ghosts. You, on the other hand, are young and beautiful and it would be a waste of your spirit. Now go," she said, squeezing Sabrina's hand. "Robert Hall is quite a catch."

"I'm not looking for romance," Sabrina said, blushing at Rose's gentle teasing.

"That's exactly when it looks for you," the old woman warned.

* * *

Early Friday evening, Sabrina stood before the cheval glass mirror in her bedroom, critically examining her outfit. She hadn't brought many clothes with her but at the last minute, she tucked a fancy cocktail dress in a suitcase. The blue strapless gown featured a sweetheart neckline and pleated bodice. A matching silk shawl complemented the tea-length gown, wrapping around her long neck and trailing softly down her back. She styled her long, dark hair casually, letting it flow over her bare shoulders. She applied a slick of lipstick and then blinked her eyes, making sure the blackened lashes were dry. No need to look like a raccoon.

She felt a thrill of panic when the doorbell rang. It had taken nearly ten years, but Robert Hall had arrived.

His eyes assessed her as she stood in the open doorway. Did he find her lacking, she wondered? He raised a corsage for her to inspect, and lifted her left hand. He slid the white rosebud onto her wrist and stepped back. Sabrina gazed at the delicate flower, attached to a diaphanous bracelet of thin, stretchy ribbon. Then her eyes lifted to measure Robert.

No, he did not lack. He wore a hand-tailored black suit,

lavender shirt and hand-painted silk tie. His short dark hair and smooth cheeks completed the image of a male model. Sabrina leaned toward him and inhaled. He even smelled like power, his tantalizing cologne stirring her senses.

"You look lovely tonight, Sabrina," he said. "Shall we go?"

Sabrina nodded and shut the door behind her, locking it and dropping the house key into her small evening bag. Robert's hand barely touched her elbow as he guided her to a sleek Audi sports car.

"Now this is lovely," she said, breathless.

"Do you like cars?" he asked.

"Well, I like this one."

As she sank into the luxurious interior, she caressed the butter-soft leather seat and admired the simple artistry of the expensive machine.

Robert slid behind the wheel, turned the ignition and the formidable motor growled. "It's only a few blocks, so we'll take it easy. But if you like, after dinner, we can take a drive to Breakthrough Lake. I'll show you how fast it can go."

Sabrina gripped her lower lip between small, white teeth. They practically glowed against the red gloss. Robert noticed and thought about her lush mouth opening beneath his.

Unaware of his tension, she continued to worry her bottom lip. "I'm a bit of a conservative, Robert," she admitted. "I don't think I would care to drive too fast."

Robert let the topic drop and within a few minutes, parked in front of the town's best Italian restaurant, Dante's. Sabrina waited for him to open her door, then she swept long legs out of the car, placed her hand in his, then stood. She flipped the matching shawl back in place, the teal band encircling her slender neck, the ends snaking down her bare back.

Oblivious to the feral look in his eyes, Sabrina clasped her purse in front of her. "I'm famished."

As they walked through the restaurant towards Robert's reserved table, he paused at a booth where a couple sat intimately sipping wine and whispering.

"Erica?"

Sabrina nearly plowed into Robert's back. Curious, she peeked around his wide shoulders at the couple and saw the friendly young woman from the bookstore.

"Robert! How nice to see you," Erica said.

He looked pointedly at the man sitting next to her.

Erica caught his message. "Oh, excuse me. This is Clay Knight. Clay, this is Robert Hall."

The man stood, nodded at Robert and extended his hand. They shook and exchanged brief greetings.

"Nice to meet you."

"Same here."

Robert, always suave and polite, stepped to the side and slid a possessive arm around Sabrina's waist. "Erica, you recall Sabrina Windham. From the bookstore," he said.

Erica nodded and smiled engagingly. Clay extended his hand again. "Nice to meet you, Sabrina."

Robert frowned, then subtly pulled Sabrina towards his chest. "Please, enjoy your dinner," he said. "I'll see you tomorrow, Erica."

Then he escorted Sabrina to his table where the restaurant owner and the waitress fawned over him.

As she studied the menu, Sabrina realized that Robert Hall led an extraordinary life, surrounded by people in awe of his breathtaking good looks and elegant style. He seemed to expect it, as if he considered it his due. It must be difficult, she thought, to be so beautiful. It's as if everyone wants a piece of him, wants to touch him, to taste him. She recalled seeing his younger sister, Katrina Hall, and having the opinion that both were so startling beautiful, they were almost unreal. She wanted to lay a comforting hand on his, but then she would be like all the rest of them. Wanting to touch him.

As dinner progressed, her heart continued to lighten

under his compliments and admiring glances but she couldn't stop thinking about leaving for Rhode Island in the morning. Her quest to find the Zephyrus took priority over her companion's charms.

Declining his offer of a late-night drive along the lakefront, Sabrina soon found herself back on the doorstep, the house key in her hand. Spending time with Robert was everything she dreamt of as a young girl, but her trip to New England dominated her thoughts. He took her hands in his, brushed his lips against her cheek and said goodnight.

"Please give Rose my best wishes. Perhaps I'll see you again while you're in town?"

Distracted, she nodded. "I will. Thank you for a lovely evening, Robert." Then she slipped inside, closing the door on her youth.

CHAPTER FOUR

Sabrina rose at six, packed an overnight bag and headed East on I-80. She estimated it would take at least six hours to get to Rhode Island, and she wanted to leave herself enough time to eat lunch and freshen up before driving to Mr. Blair's house. Her stomach twisted. This kind of impetuous behavior wasn't normal for her. She left spontaneity and reckless impulse to her parents.

She turned on the radio, hoping the diversion would settle her anxiety. Unaccustomed to driving in traffic, she was a bundle of nerves by the time she crossed the Tappan Zee Bridge in New York. "It's all downhill from here," she told herself. Then she hit the Connecticut traffic on I-95.

She snarled. "Where do all these people come from? It's not even rush hour."

Instead of six hours, the drive took eight. She pulled into Warren around two o'clock, her stomach rumbling from hunger. She drove south on Route 136, Market Street, looking for a café. She didn't want fast food; she needed to sit in a booth and eat slowly, waiting for the roar in her ears to subside. She drove past a cheery blue-and-white wooden sign with a sailboat and arrow. It read

"Warren Boatyard." In the distance, the Warren River twinkled. She spotted piers and white boats behind many houses. Finally, she found a small coffee shop and pulled in. The Cadillac's large engine hissed when she turned off the ignition.

Sabrina closed her eyes, savoring the quiet. She drove straight through, stopping only once at a rest area in Matamoras, Pennsylvania. It was a nerve-wracking experience for a city girl whose jaunts were measured in blocks.

For a Saturday afternoon, the small town was quiet. A young couple walked their terrier down the sidewalk, and a lone man sat outside the coffee shop reading a newspaper. Sabrina picked up her purse and got out of the car. She wasn't sure if she should lock it.

Silly; this isn't Baltimore, she thought.

Inside the small restaurant, she sank into a comfy booth and picked up the cardboard menu. She selected a fresh garden salad, a bowl of mushroom barley soup, a multi-grain roll, and a strawberry smoothie from the eclectic menu. "This is wonderful," she gushed, spooning the last of the soup into her mouth before the waitress could clear the dishes. "I haven't had soup like this since … um, never."

"It's a specialty of ours. We make the best soups in town. No kidding. You should try the fudge, too. Killer," the waitress said, winking.

"I will. Thanks," she said. "Is it always this quiet? I'm visiting from out of town."

"Well, it's too late for the lunch crowd but it's not normally this deserted," she said, looking out the large front window.

Sabrina paid her bill, left a large tip and took along a serving of fudge for later. She drove by the hotel and, since it was after three o'clock, checked into her room. She stashed her suitcase beside the bed and took few minutes to wash her face, freshen her makeup and brush her hair.

She changed into a pair of jeans and sneakers, recalling that Mr. Blair said the boat was stored near a barn. She grabbed her lightweight black leather coat, and brushed breadcrumbs off her maroon tailored shirt. She tugged at the V-neck, now worried that it was too low and too tight.

"I hope he doesn't think I'm making a pass at him," she said to her reflection. She double checked her teeth for stray flecks of pepper, then slid her hotel key card into her back pocket.

Back in the Cadillac, Sabrina looked at the directions, wishing she'd brought a state map along instead of a one-page computer printout. The instructions to his house were clear, but what if she made a wrong turn? How would she make it back to the starting point? She shrugged, and started the car.

Traffic was still light, and she offered a brief prayer of thanks. A few minutes later, after turning right, checking the directions, turning left, checking them again, and trying to keep her eye on her mileage (how the heck can you go 1.7 miles?), she stopped the car in front of a small, battered two-story house. In the distance, she saw a barn. Behind that, the Warren River sparkled.

She pulled into the unpaved driveway and parked a few yards from a sagging front porch. As she stepped out of the car, Mr. Blair, a bent old man in overalls and a faded, plaid shirt, ambled down the porch steps.

"Good afternoon," he rasped. "You the Windham girl I talked with the other day?"

"Yes sir," she said, extending her hand. His grasp was strong and his blue eyes twinkled.

"You're a pretty little thing, aren't you?"

"It's nice to meet you, Mr. Blair." She gestured with a nod to the barn. "Is the Zephyrus over there?"

"Ah yup. Guess you're anxious to see it, aren't you?"

"I am. I'm very excited. I've never seen one of my grandfather's boats."

"Eh? Why not?"

"After he died, my grandmother moved to the mountains of Pennsylvania. I live in Baltimore, and don't have much time for recreation."

"That's too bad. Coming from a sailing family as you do, you should have blue water in your veins. Well, come on along."

He shuffled through the tall grass, his feet finding the path to the barnyard. Sabrina cringed when the small old man pushed against a heavy wooden gate. She thought she should lend a shoulder, but then the gate creaked and swung open. Chickens cackled and raced out the opening of the barn.

"Don't mind them. They like to nap in here," Blair said.

In the shadows on the side of the barn, covered with several faded and torn canvas tarps, she could make out a large lump that must be the sailboat. She tiptoed towards it, unsure what might be living inside. Blair wasn't as shy. He strode forward and yanked the tarps off the boat.

Sabrina gasped. It sat in a rusted, steel cradle, and its broken lead keel lay beside it. It was chalky white, with black streaks running down the hull. The bent mast lay across the cockpit, crushing the bow pulpit. Varnish peeled off the faded teak trim.

She looked closer. There were bales of moldy hay on the cockpit seats and she could hear the "cheep cheep" of tiny peeps in the cabin.

Blair plucked a ladder from the side of the barn and leaned it against the boat hull with a thud. "Help yourself, missy. Have a good look."

"I'm not sure what to look for," she murmured.

"Well, what is it you want to know?"

"I'm searching for Hull Number One; the first boat my grandfather made. Your invoice was the earliest, and I was hoping that maybe this boat …," her voice faded.

"Well, what you gotta do is climb up in there and look in the cabin. There's a bronze builder's plate on one of the bulkheads. That's where it tells you the hull number. Why do you want Hull Number One?"

"A personal quest, I guess you could say."

He stepped back. "Like I said, help yourself."

Sabrina climbed the ladder and stepped gingerly into the cockpit. She looked over the edge. "In there?"

"Ayuh."

She inched towards the cabin opening and removed a warped teak washboard. "Do you have a flashlight?"

"Nope. I have a lighter. Want it?"

"Um, sure. Thanks." She caught the deftly tossed stainless steel Zippo lighter. She flipped the lid and timidly rubbed the wheel. After a few tries, the spark caught igniting a small butane flame. She leaned inside the cabin and looked around. It was filled with several inches of black, oily water. Chicken feathers floated on the surface.

"Where did this water come from?" she called over her shoulder.

"Hatch leaks."

She didn't want to step into the rank water, so she leaned farther and reached her arm forward, the flame casting shadows on the washed-out teak. The lighter was growing hot, beginning to burn her fingers. She couldn't see a bronze plate. She almost gave up, had pulled her hand back toward her face when out of the corner of her eye she saw it. It was on the bulkhead by the cabin opening. She clung to the teak grab rails and bent at the waist, twisting to see the plate.

It read, "Zephyrus 32, No. 1, Zephyrus Yachts, Warren, Rhode Island."

"Yes!" she whispered.

As she backed down the ladder, she wished she could ask Rose what to do next.

Mr. Blair stood to the side, chewing a piece of hay, his eyebrows lifted in amusement.

She didn't know how to buy a boat, didn't know what kind of questions to ask. She started with the most important.

"I want to buy it. Will you sell?"

"Well, you see, I'm fond of that boat."

"But you haven't taken care of it. You can't sail it. Why would you want to keep it?"

"I don't. I'm just warming up."

"I don't understand. You do want to sell the boat, then?"

"Maybe. How much?"

"I don't know. What's a boat like that worth?"

"It's worth $5,000 to me."

"What? That's what you paid thirty years ago. I know, I've got the invoice," she said, her voice incredulous.

"That's what it's worth. Do you want it?" The canny old man leaned against the Cadillac and squinted at her.

"Yes."

"Then we gotta deal," he said, sticking out his hand.

Sabrina cautiously shook it. "Will you accept a check?"

The old man looked at her car, then her, then the car again. "Sure."

CHAPTER FIVE

Back at the hotel, Sabrina called Rose. "It's here, Grandmother. I've found it."

"How exciting. I bet she's beautiful."

"Not really. It's been stored next to a barn for a long time, and it looks pretty shabby right now."

"Boats are female, so you must refer to the Zephyrus properly. Calling her an 'it' is not nice."

Sabrina chuckled. "Boat etiquette, huh?"

"Correct. Now that you're an owner, you have to follow protocol."

"That's right; we own a sailboat. I gave that old thief a check today. What should I do now, Grandmother? I must get it repaired. I mean 'her' repaired."

"Find a local boatyard and talk to the owner. They can arrange to have it transported to their shop."

"It's going to be more expensive than I thought," Sabrina warned.

"I'm sure it will be," Rose replied, "but it's a labor of love, darling. It's worth it."

"I don't know if it's a blessing or a blight, but I'm glad I have you and that you understand."

"It's a blessing. Goodbye, dear."

Sabrina turned off her cell phone and walked to the window. She lifted the gauze curtain and looked at the Warren River shimmering nearby. She relived her adventure, marveling at all she'd accomplished in one day. Then her stomach growled. So much for the satisfying soup and salad. It was tasty, but it wasn't filling. Picking up her purse and leather coat, she headed out, stopping in the lobby to ask the clerk for directions to a nearby restaurant.

"Preferably something close. Walking distance," she emphasized.

The man crinkled his forehead. "Well, there's the donut shop, but that's not real food. If you go three blocks that way, you'll come to a little bar called Maude's," he said, pointing out the glass front door. "It looks like a dive on the outside, but the food is great. It's still early so there won't be a crowd."

"Thanks," she said, and strutted out the hotel. She felt jubilant, she felt alive. She never had adventures or took risks, and she had done both today. No matter the outcome, she enjoyed finding the sailboat and promised herself that she would never regret it.

She heard the music before she saw the bar. It was a weather-beaten building with several motorcycles and pickup trucks in the parking lot. A neon sign glowed in the window advertising a popular beer from a small-town Pennsylvania brewery not far from Eaton. She opened the door and walked in.

The interior was a contrast in light and dark: well-lit over the pool table where two men concentrated on their game, dim along the far wall, lined with wooden booths. The bar stools were filled with people Sabrina imagined were "regulars." She nodded to the bartender and headed for an empty booth. As she sat down, she plopped her purse on the table and slipped out of her coat.

Across the bar, Jay West sipped his beer, keeping his

narrowed eyes pinned on the young woman. As soon as she walked in, he noticed the exotic beauty with dark hair and delicate features. His gaze wandered to luscious cleavage when she slipped off her coat. She smiled, her toothy grin bright against red lipstick, when the bartender stumbled in his haste to bring her a menu.

The stunning girl exuded refinement and money. What was she doing in Warren and, more important, was she alone?

Nate, the bartender, nodded as she handed him back the menu and asked for a beer and a cheeseburger.

Jay's upper lip curled into a wolfish grin.

"Hey, are you listening to me?"

Jay glanced at the heavy-set man on the stool next to him. While Brett's wife, Shawna, held a scrapbooking workshop at their house, he relaxed with a beer and dinner at Maude's.

"No," Jay replied.

Brett looked around, curious until he spotted Sabrina. "Whoa brother; she's out of your league."

On the other side of the bar, Sabrina noticed the tall man sitting on a stool. He was dressed in a faded black T-shirt, and his rough, worn jeans rode up his ankles, revealing a pair of scuffed work boots. Chestnut hair curled over his ears and flipped up at the back of his neck. A lock strayed into eyes framed with dark, flaring brows. It was a hip fashion that pretentious executives paid hundreds of dollars to achieve, yet this man's style sprang from nonchalance.

High cheekbones slashed his face and the beginnings of a short beard and mustache muted his mouth. A fisherman? Probably a construction worker, she thought. Still, he's sexy.

She grinned a bit too brightly at the bartender, thanking him for the beer. Nervous, she hefted the bottle and bumped her front tooth. Clunk.

"Ouch," she murmured, rubbing her front teeth with

her index finger, worried she chipped one. She glanced at the bar and met Jay's eyes. Was he smiling at her?

She lifted the longneck and drank, her throat undulating with each gulp, then set the beer on the table and wiped her mouth with the back of her hand. She was aware of his eyes on her and her skin tingled. She gazed at her bottle and tugged nervously at the label, a game bored females play at bars. Soon, shreds of wet paper littered the tabletop, but it worked. The time between placing her order and having a hot, juicy burger placed before her dissolved.

"Yes, please," she responded to the bartender's question. "Ketchup and mustard. Thanks."

She lifted the bun lid and poked at the burger. Hot cheese clung to her finger and she slid it into her mouth, sucking it clean. As she pulled her finger from her lips, she looked up and once again saw the intent man watching her. Blushing with embarrassment, she shifted in her seat and knocked her purse onto the floor. As she bent to retrieve it, she watched in agony as a tube of lipstick rolled across the floor, bouncing off the barstool next to the man. Sabrina pretended she hadn't noticed it and shoved the rest of the contents back into her purse. She decided she would buy another lipstick, considering the tube lost.

Meanwhile, Nate brought the ketchup and mustard and hovered at her table. "Can I get you another beer, miss?"

"Thank you. That'd be great," she said.

She refused to look across the bar, determined to eat her burger, drink her beer and leave while she still had some dignity. She didn't understand why she felt self-conscious, but after a few minutes of trying to eat daintily, she gave up and devoured the sandwich.

To hell with him, she thought. He's rude, staring at me like that.

Agitated, she chewed, her cheeks stuffed with bread and meat. The burger was no longer juicy. It was cardboard, dry and tasteless. She gulped her second beer, washing down the last few mouthfuls.

Pulling her wallet from her purse, she extracted a fifty-dollar bill and placed it on the table. She was furious. The entire time she tried to eat her dinner, minding her own business, the obnoxious man at the bar stared at her. Okay, so she licked her finger suggestively and a few times, she stared back at him, but enough was enough.

She grabbed her purse and jacket and swung out of the booth. "Keep the change," she told the bartender, whose mouth gaped in astonishment at the size of the tip.

In the parking lot, Sabrina slipped into her coat and hung her purse over her shoulder. She turned in a slow circle, unsure which direction the hotel lay. As she did, the tavern door opened. Jay walked out and stopped in front of her. In his open hand, he held her lipstick. She glared at it for a heated moment, and then considered his face. It was shadowed, except for his lower lip. She fixated on it.

"I hope you're happy. You've ruined my night out."

"Me?" His voice was low and soft.

Dangerous, she thought.

"Yes, you," she lashed, grabbing the lipstick and shoving it in her front pocket. "Who do you think you are, staring at me?"

"You were flirting with me."

Sabrina took a step back and gasped. "I was not! I was trying to enjoy dinner, but I couldn't because of you."

Jay stepped closer forcing Sabrina to lift her chin to see him. It exposed the long, pale line of her neck. He hungrily followed that line to the swell of her breasts, heaving against the too-tight shirt. Jay also saw a wisp of dark lace. "You fooled me."

"You're incredibly rude and you're making me nervous." Sabrina took another step back.

He pushed his hands into his jeans pocket and grinned. "Let's start over. I'm Jay; what's your name?"

"None of your business," she snapped, anxiously turning her head, looking for the hotel sign.

He touched her arm gently. "Hey, it's okay. Are you lost?"

Sabrina looked up into his shadowed face, wishing she could see his eyes. She forced herself to calm down. She was in the parking lot of a brightly lit restaurant in the tiny town of Warren, not a dark alley in Baltimore. "I'm not sure where my hotel is. It's only a few blocks away, but I don't remember which way to go."

"I'll walk with you. It's probably the Warren Inn, right?"

"Yes, but you don't need to walk with me. Which way is it?"

"This way," he said, turning her, his hand gentle on her elbow.

Sabrina took several steps toward what she hoped would be her hotel, then stopped. She looked pointedly at his hand on her arm, then at his face. She blinked in surprise. This time, light from the waning sun revealed a scattering of freckles across a straight nose, a full mouth with straight, white teeth. His eyes weren't dark after all; they were clear gray-blue. Glints of red shone in his mussed hair.

He released her arm.

Sabrina caught her bottom lip between her teeth. From a distance, he was hard lines and angles, but now, outside in the fading light, he was almost adorable.

Without thinking, Sabrina lifted her hand in a halting gesture. Jay caught it and gently held it between them.

"All right, maybe I was flirting. At first," she conceded. "But not now. I don't know you. I think I'd better go." Shakily, Sabrina pulled her hand away.

"I'd like to know you," he said. "What's your name?"

This time she couldn't refuse. With bright eyes pinned on his lips, she answered breathlessly. "Sabrina."

"Sabrina, you're the most beautiful woman I've ever seen."

"Yeah, right," she drawled.

"I never lie." He glanced over her shoulder, then changed the subject. "It's going to be a nice evening. Would you like to go for a sunset sail?"

Sabrina blinked again. "What?"

"Take a short sail on the river and watch the sunset," he explained. "It's a Rhode Island tradition."

"I've never been on a sailboat before."

Well, except for this afternoon, but that doesn't count, she mentally added.

He gestured to a large, vacant lot across the street. On the far side of the lot, along the river, several small sailboats bobbed at a pier. "Here's your chance."

She frowned, but the idea of sailing, even with a stranger, intrigued her. "How do I know you're not a murderer? That you're not going to dump by body in the bay?"

"You don't, but this is a small town and everyone knows me. I can give you a reference."

As if on cue, an older couple walked out of the bar and headed for a truck in the parking lot. "Good evening Jay," they called.

"Good evening Paul, Barb," he replied, his eyes pinned on Sabrina.

"That was convenient," she said.

"I'll take that as a yes." He sheathed her hand in his, its heat radiating up her arm. They crossed the street in silence, walking towards the boats rocking in the current.

"Which one is yours?" she asked, tugging her hand free.

Jay nimbly dropped into a small boat and patted the gunwale. "They all are. But this evening, we'll use this one. She's my favorite. Just give me a minute to get her ready, then you can climb aboard."

Sabrina watched as he tugged on the shrouds, making sure that the rigging was tight. He pulled the cover off the mainsail and checked the sail ties. He placed the rudder in the water and tied the tiller against the port side of the boat, then stood in the cockpit and looked around.

"Ready?" she asked.

"Wait just a sec. Going over my list," he said, then continued his mental survey. After checking in the small cabin for life jackets and flares, he stepped to the middle of the boat and held out his hand, beckoning Sabrina.

She gingerly put her fingertips in his hand, then stepped onto the seat cushion. The boat rocked and she grabbed his arm with both hands. Jay pulled her towards the middle of the cockpit and the motion stopped.

"You've never sailed before?"

"I told you I hadn't. This is a small boat, isn't it?"

"Yes, but it's fast and fun. I promise you won't go for a swim tonight."

"I'd better not," she warned, sitting on the cushion and placing her purse beside her. She squiggled out of her coat, the movement again catching Jay's eye as her shirt stretched across her breasts.

He looked away, then reached out of the boat and released the lines from the pier. He pulled in the fenders and stowed them in the small cabin. Using the boat hook, he shoved the dinghy away from the pilings and they were adrift. Not bothering to use the small outboard motor, Jay maneuvered the boat into the wind.

"Would you please sit here and hold the tiller like this?" He offered Sabrina the teak handle.

"Why? Aren't you going to sail the boat?"

"Yes, but I need to raise the sail. Unless you want to do it?"

"No thanks," she said reaching for the tiller. "I'll hold the thingy."

Jay stood and deftly untied the sail. Within seconds, he shackled the top of it to the halyard and pulled the bright white nylon up the mast. Unabashed, Sabrina watched as the muscles in his back rippled. He cleated the line, then unfurled the jib sheet. The small sail curved and filled with the slight breeze.

"Okay, we're ready to go," he said, smiling. He took the tiller from Sabrina and sat on the opposite side of the boat. "Just sit back and relax."

"Great idea," she said. But could she relax? She'd been impetuous, agreeing to go sailing with a stranger. A rugged and sexy stranger with beautiful, strong hands she realized as she watched him steer the little boat into open water. The sensation of letting go and being uninhibited for once thrilled her.

The little dinghy moved quickly in the light wind. Sabrina watched the shoreline recede, and admired the houses and yachts as the boat forged down the Warren River toward the bay.

"We won't go far," Jay said. "It's nice, though, to have a stretch of water between you and the sunset."

Sabrina closed her eyes. She reveled in the warmth of the setting sun and the gentle breeze. The water was nearly flat, so the small waves rippled in the boat's wake.

"This is wonderful," she said, her face tilted towards the breeze. "I've never experienced anything like this."

"Don't you like boats?" Jay asked.

"Well, sure. I've just never had the opportunity to go on one. I mean, in school I joined the crew club, but that's rowing on the river. It's more about competition than relaxation. I've been on a couple of dinner cruises on the Patapsco River."

"You live near the Chesapeake Bay?"

He knows his geography, she thought. "Yes. I live in Baltimore."

"Busy place. Do you like it there?"

"Well, sure. I've lived there most of my life, so it's home. I went to boarding school in Maryland."

"You went to a boarding school?"

"Yes. Good old Hillcrest. Class of 1998. Then I went to Boston for college."

"Boston as in…?"

"As in Harvard Business School. Yes, I'm a nerd."

"You don't look like the nerds I went to school with." Jay observed.

Sabrina dimpled at the compliment and Jay lost his heart.

"Where did you go to school?" she asked.

"I was born here and went to public school. Then I moved to Maine, worked at a few boatyards there and got my degree in naval architecture at the Maine Maritime Academy."

"Architecture? You build houses?"

Jay laughed gently at her naiveté. "No, I design boats."

"Really?" Sabrina squeaked. "My grandfather ....," she began, then yelped and grabbed at his knees when a large wake rocked the dinghy.

"Careful," Jay said, steadying her. "There's a couple more coming. They're from that tug over there," he pointed.

Sabrina placed her hands on either side, balancing herself. "Sorry; I wasn't expecting that."

"Would you like to steer?" Jay offered.

"No thanks. If you don't mind, I'd rather watch the sunset," she said. "It is beautiful, isn't it?"

Jay nodded as the sun sank closer to the horizon. Orange, pink and violet banded together for the spectacular event. As the sun sank into the bay, Jay turned the boat and headed back towards the river, tacking slowly towards Warren.

Sabrina watched as he handled the sheets and tiller with expertise, and all too soon the experience ended. Jay handed her the tiller and told her to keep the boat steady while he pulled down the mainsail and tied it to the boom. He let the current move them to the pier and then tossed a line around a piling.

He held her hand as she stood on the seat and jumped to the pier. She dropped a loop around a cleat as instructed and waited as Jay finished docking the boat. Soon, the small vessel was secure, its fenders cushioning it from the weathered pilings. He tossed the life jackets into the cabin, tidied up the lines and lifted the rudder from the water. He slid the cover back on the flaked mainsail, nodding as he mentally checked items on his list.

He sprang to the pier and stood next to Sabrina in the dusk. "Hope that makes up for staring at you in the bar."

She laughed. "I've forgotten all about that." She bit her bottom lip, suppressing a smirk and dimpling instead.

There it is, again, Jay thought and before he could stop he said, "I've been dying to kiss you."

She felt heat radiate from him as she swayed. He's hypnotized me, she thought, and closed her eyes. When their mouths touched, his gentle and hesitant, she dove recklessly. She sought his kiss with lush, full lips, leaning into him when the ground tilted.

Jay wrapped his arms around her and caressed her back and neck. His fingers slid into her dark hair as she deepened the kiss, giving her time to explore, to experiment. When she sucked on his bottom lip, nipping it gently with her sharp, white teeth, Jay knew he had to stop her while he still could.

He pulled back. "Whoa," he murmured. "Now I can die a happy man."

She buried her face in his chest, embarrassed by her wanton exuberance.

As her head cleared, she heard an incessant barking and honking. She pulled away, swiveling her head. "What's that noise?"

Jay lifted her chin and rubbed his thumb against her bottom lip. "Seals. We get a lot of seals in Rhode Island. They come up the bay in the fall, but we've got a few early ones. If you'd like, I'll show you. There's a group sleeping on the rocks," he said, pointing in the direction opposite the hotel.

"Sure," she said. "Why not?" Although honestly, she knew why not.

They walked along the river towards a wooden

complex surrounded by a high chain-link fence. As promised, seals lounged on a collection of flat rocks at the edge of the river. At the sound of their footsteps rustling the grass, a few wary seals lifted their heads and barked. One began to shake.

"We're too close," Jay said and drew Sabrina back a few feet.

Once the seals were appeased by the distance, they reclined, keeping their bright eyes on the humans.

"Can we watch them for a while? Do you mind?" Sabrina asked.

"Sure. Let's sit down here."

She sat cross-legged in the grass, keeping as still as possible while watching the seals. Soon, their snoozing relaxed her and she leaned back on her elbows. She looked at the dark sky, searching for constellations she could recognize. It was a futile gesture, so she gazed at Jay.

"Now you're staring," he teased.

"Sorry. The grass is wet and I'm cold," she confessed.

"Let's go," he said, standing and offering a hand.

"Where are we going?"

"My place. I'll loan you a towel," he said.

"This is where you murder me?"

He laughed softly. "Trust me."

"That's what they all say," Sabrina retorted, but she kept her fingers wrapped in his and hiked around the fence toward the wooden complex.

"Watch your step," he said, leading her up a wooden staircase. A motion detector on the building lit the area. Sabrina noticed gray cedar shingles beyond stairs, that ended on a deck that faced the river.

Jay opened a door and flipped a light switch. "Would you like to come in?"

Hesitant, Sabrina stepped into the sparsely decorated loft apartment, trimmed in teak and brass like the inside of a sailboat. The curtains were made of old canvas sails and prints of majestic tall ships adorned the walls. An oversized couch covered in dark blue ultra-suede dominated the room, partitioned by a gleaming, mahogany bar. Behind it was a small, tidy kitchenette with polished nickel appliances. Jay picked up a remote and turned on a receiver, tuning it to a radio station playing rock music.

"You really like sailboats, don't you?" Sabrina asked, turning in a full circle as she admired the space.

"No. I love sailboats," he emphasized, handing her a hand towel. "Can I get you a drink?"

"Sure. Water, please. I like sailboats, too. In fact, I bought one today. I can't believe I just said that. I bought a boat."

"Hey, that's great. Welcome to my world." He handed her a bottle of water and touched her elbow. "Let's sit down and you can tell me about it."

While he unlaced his boots, and tossed them in a corner, Sabrina sat and twisted the bottle cap. The water was cool and refreshing. Sitting a short distance from her, he lifted her legs and tugged off her shoes. He swung her feet into his lap, spinning her to face him. With a light touch, he massaged the soles of her feet.

Breathing was difficult, and she shivered. Uncertainty made her wary.

"So, who are you Sabrina, and what brought you here?"

Emboldened, she teased him. "Here? You mean, to your lair?"

He grinned wolfishly.

"Wait," she protested, pulling her feet from his lap. She sat straight and placed her bottle on the table. "I'm not sure what's going on here, but, umm ..." She looked around helplessly. Telling him about the Zephyrus was the last thing on her mind.

Jay watched her struggle with anxiety and leaned back against the couch, one hand resting on his knee, the other framing his head. The effect was one of submission, opening his body and assuring her that she was in control.

It was a natural, inviting gesture and one her body

recognized instinctively, whether or not she understood. She slid against him, wrapping her arms around his neck. "Don't make me talk anymore. Kiss me." She closed her eyes and waited.

Amused, Jay stroked her hair from her face and lifted her chin. He brushed her lips with his. She grunted a protest and wiggled deeper into his arms. "Kiss me," she demanded, her eyes still closed.

His mouth was hot as it melded with hers, and oh, could he kiss. He pulled her against him, making her head swim at the contact. She sucked tenderly on his bottom lip, inviting him into aggression. He fisted his hands in her hair and pulled her head to the side, baring her neck and shoulder. With a growl, he plundered and Sabrina gasped at the bolt of desire she felt.

This animal need was new; never had she been so reckless or daring. Or so frightened.

She pushed against his chest, shaking her head. "Stop. No, um, thank you," she said. "I, um, I need to go now."

Jay released her and sank against the cushions. "Are you sure? I didn't mean to upset you."

Sabrina stood, smoothing her shirt. She tucked it back into her jeans, then reached for her shoes. She swayed as stood on one foot, cramming her toes into the laced-up sneaker.

"I'm not upset," she lied. "I'm fine. I need to go." The words came out in a jumble as she fumbled with her other shoe.

"Can I see you again?"

She paused at the door, her hand resting on the knob. "No, I'm sorry. I'm leaving tomorrow. Thank you for the sunset sail. Goodbye," she said, her voice prim and polite.

Bemused, Jay watched as she fled into the night, slamming the door behind her.

She shivered in the night air as she backtracked down the stairs, around the fence and back to the street. Guilt clouded her thoughts. Making out with a perfect stranger.

She could blame it on alcohol, although she'd only had two beers at the most. No, it wasn't alcohol. It was the sunset and the sailor's carefree, lazy smile.

CHAPTER SIX

In the morning, the town once again seemed normal. Sabrina shook her head at the memory of her race through the dark streets. Although Jay lived somewhere close to the hotel and the tavern, she'd lost all sense of bearing in the dark. He could be anywhere. Not that she wanted to see him again. Okay, she did, but she didn't think she could face him.

She need to stay on target. Her immediate plan was to move the boat to a reliable boatyard and then return to Eaton and Grandmother Rose. She didn't need the complication of a one-night stand.

He's probably glad he doesn't have to get rid of me, she thought. *I've got the morals of a cat in heat.*

A vision of Sister Carolyn, her seventh-grade health education teacher, floated before her. She cringed at the memory of sex education and the Catholic stance on reproduction and birth control. That's where she and the religion parted ways. In most other areas, the doctrine had its hooks in her and kept her on the "right path."

Even so, Sabrina had limited experience with sex. She dated during high school, but never had a serious relationship.

She'd only made love with two other men: one she almost convinced herself to marry, despite Grandmother Rose's advice, and the other a rebound from her broken engagement.

She dated Jeremy Rice for three years in college. He took it for granted they would marry and she would work while he finished medical school. Finding him in bed with another woman at a fraternity party devastated her. Jeremy represented the one thing she craved: a family. She refused his contrite telephone calls and eventually they stopped. She sent him the engagement ring and returned all his presents. She didn't want any reminders.

Michael, her second lover, was a guitar player in a Boston band. Her dorm roommate set up a blind date for both. They recognized from the beginning they had little in common, but the sex was healthy and helped assuage her wounded pride. Michael didn't mind. When his band moved to California, they kissed goodbye without regret.

Sabrina was up, showered and dressed by eight o'clock, and scouting the streets of Warren for a breakfast diner. She decided on the donut shop, eating three glazed donuts and downing a large cup of coffee.

She asked the waitress for a telephone directory and idly stirred sugar into her coffee as she flipped through the yellow pages.

"Excuse me," she called to the waitress. "Is this close?" Sabrina pointed to the small ad for Warren Boatyard in the phone book. Its services included boat restoration and boat building, "no job too small."

The woman nodded. "Sure is. Right down the road."

"Thanks. That's all I need."

Sabrina punched the number into her cell phone. It rang several times. Just as she considered hanging up and redialing, a deep voice boomed, "Boatyard. Brett here."

"Hello, I'm looking at your ad in the phone book and it says you do boat restoration. That 'no job is too small.' "

"That's right, ma'am. What can we do for you?"

"Well, I have a boat and it's a real mess," she began apologetically. "I need to have it moved and then, I guess, do whatever magic you do."

"Is this a fiberglass boat?"

"Yes, it is."

"What's her length, overall?"

"Uh, what?"

"How big is the boat?"

"I'm not sure. It's a Zephyrus; does that help?"

There was a brief pause before the man answered. "Thirty-two; those boats had a short run and only one design."

"Well, this one is special, despite roosting chickens and lily pads in living room."

"Cabin. Lily pads in the cabin," Brett said, chuckling. "Where is this boat?"

"It's at Mr. Blair's house, next to his barn." She reeled off the address. "It's been sitting for at least twenty years, so it's going to need a lot of work."

"I can go look at it and give you an estimate. Why don't you give me your name and telephone number?"

"I don't need an estimate. I want this boat restored to her original condition," she said, proudly remembering to call it by its feminine pronoun. "I don't care what the cost is."

Brett didn't respond at first. Then, "Miss, you sound like you're new to sailboats. Let me give you some advice: When you fall in love, run like hell."

"Excuse me?" Sabrina's gut clenched.

"Run, and don't look back. This boat could end up costing you ten times what she's worth."

"That's what she's worth to me," Sabrina said. "Look; you're right. I don't know what I'm doing. That's why I'm calling you. But I do know this: I want this boat in pristine condition."

"Bristol."

"What?"

"Bristol. Boats are restored to Bristol condition, not pristine."

She giggled. "Whatever, Mr. ... What did you say your name was?"

"My name is Brett Story. I'm assistant manager of the Warren Boatyard."

"Mr. Story, I appreciate you trying to talk me out of throwing money at you. You may not hear this often, but today, money is no object. In fact, if you'll meet me at Mr. Blair's house with a truck or trailer, or however you people move boats around on the land, then I'm prepared to give you a $20,000 deposit."

"I can be there in an hour."

Not a bad businessman after all, she thought.

"That's what I want to hear. Thank you, Mr. Story."

Sabrina hung up her cell phone. "I'm doing it, Grandmother," she said aloud.

Next, she called the hospital and talked to Shirley Piper, her grandmother's personal nurse.

"She's doing very well, Sabrina. In fact, we're beginning physical therapy today. We need to get her moving so her hip mends properly. The doctors say it was a small fracture and she's ready to try the walker."

"Thank you, Shirley. I appreciate what you've done for her. May I speak with her?"

"She's having a sponge bath right now and then will eat breakfast. Can you call back in about an hour?"

"Sure. Well it will have to be a little later. I'm going to pick up my new boat."

"How nice! You bought a new boat?"

"Well, not really new. But she will be like new when she's finished."

Sabrina signed off and looked at the small clock on her cell phone. It was a little after nine; she called Mr. Blair and arranged to meet him again, this time with a mover.

"That'll be fine, missy. You might want to come over here a little sooner and get rid of the peeps. Unless you want some chickens."

"Mr. Blair, surely you will remove your property from my boat."

"I would if I could, girly, but I can't climb no ladder and my eyesight isn't what it used to be."

Sabrina gritted her teeth. Fine, she thought, you old crook.

Sabrina bailed many buckets of greasy, black water from the cabin, removed three hen's nests, and tossed eight bales of hay from the boat by the time Brett Story arrived. He efficiently maneuvered a tractor-trailer next to the barn. He climbed onto the truck bed, removed chains from a forklift and drove it down the ramp, parking it by the sailboat. Then he hopped off to study the Zephyrus.

Once Brett had weighed his options, he guided the long, padded blades of the forklift under the sailboat and lifted it, swinging it effortlessly onto the long tractor bed. Once again, Brett hopped off the forklift and then slung several webbed straps across the boat, cinching it to the trailer. Next he deposited the broken lead keel in front of the boat, then drove the little forklift back up the ramp and attached the chains, securing it to the tractor-trailer.

The process took less than twenty minutes. Looking at Sabrina, he shook his head. "You sure you want to do this?"

She handed him a check for $20,000. "I'm sure."

Now that he had the boat secure, Brett took a moment to study Sabrina. "Didn't I see you last night at Maude's? Weren't you ... uh, didn't you and ..."

He stammered, suddenly realizing the awkwardness of the situation.

Sabrina's cheeks reddened. "Maybe. I had dinner there last night," she said, looking away. "I'm Sabrina Windham and this boat was designed and built by my grandfather, Don Windham," she added, pride flushing her cheeks.

Brett stared open-mouthed.

Sabrina waited for another response. Brett's silence filled the gap.

"Well, my grandfather and his partner, Derek West," she amended. "I'm determined this boat will be restored and, like I said, I don't care what it costs. It's that important."

Brett exhaled. "Right. Well, guess I'll be off. I'm going to need you to come by the boatyard this afternoon to sign some paperwork. No matter what you say, the boss will insist on an estimate. He's particular about the paperwork." Brett eyed the Zephyrus warily. "I think he's going to want to deal with you, and your boat, personally."

"No problem. What time is best for you?"

Brett stepped up to the truck cab and opened the door. "I'd say after three. We've got to do a survey first. Then we can write up a list of priorities."

She would have to delay leaving town for another day, but she needed to get the boat transferred and a plan for restoration in place.

"That will fine. I'll see you then," Sabrina said, eyeing the chalky, swollen belly of her boat. Without the keel, the boat sat cradled between two massive wood blocks on the trailer. She grinned once more at Brett. "Too late I'm afraid to 'run like hell.' "

"They do get under your skin. Kinda like a woman. Well, not in your case. Maybe. Uhhh, I better get a move on before I put my foot deeper in my mouth."

She winked at him. "Men; I prefer men. With one exception," she said, gazing at the boat once more.

Sabrina stood beside Mr. Blair in the overgrown weeds in his front yard as Brett drove the 18-wheeler out of the barnyard.

He shook his head as the truck disappeared down the road.

"Well, missy, you got yourself some project there."

CHAPTER SEVEN

Jay was in the machine shop, the radio blasting loud rock music when Brett returned with the loaded truck. He didn't hear the engine or the air brakes over the music and the grinding wheel that he operated, shaping a new engine mount. A rag tossed at his head alerted him to Brett's presence.

"Where have you been?" he growled.

"Working, which is more than I can say for you," Brett countered. "Wish I could drag my lazy ass to work whenever I wanted."

"Yeah, well I misplaced something this morning."

"Wouldn't be a sexy brunette, would it?"

Jay tossed the rag at Brett. "Mind your own business. What's that?" he gestured to the laden truck.

"That, my friend, is our next project. I've got a check for $20,000 and I need a survey and estimate quick."

Jay stepped out of the attached shed and into the yard. He recognized the boat immediately, swiveling to glare at Brett.

"What the hell is this?"

"It's a Zephyrus, buddy."

"I can see that. What the hell is it doing here?"

"Picked it up this morning down on Route 136. Customer wants it restored to Bristol. Says she will pay whatever it takes. This here twenty grand deposit," he said, patting his shirt pocket, "is a down payment."

"Well, I don't want it. Get rid of it."

"Come on, Jay. Get real; we can use the work and you know it. Besides, this is a project boat. We restore this classic and we'll get some great publicity. Think what Shawna can do with the web site. We'll put photos of before and after. It'll be great."

"I don't want it here. I'm not going to touch this boat," Jay snarled. "Get it out of here."

"Well, Jay, here's the thing. This boat just happens to be Hull Number One of a design by Don Windham and his partner, Derek West. You are West's grandson and, here is the clincher, the new owner is the granddaughter of Don Windham."

Jay swore viciously and picked up a piece of two-by-four. In a rage, he swung at the boat. The dull gel coat cracked.

"Jay, calm down. Man, this is Karma. Don't you see?"

"No, I don't see."

"You will. It gets better. The granddaughter is a sexy brunette named Sabrina."

This took the wind from Jay's sail and he stepped back, tripping over the dropped board and sitting hard on a box of old canvas.

"Knocked you on your ass, didn't I?"

Jay swore viciously, then stood up, wiped the sawdust from his jeans and walked to the back lot where seals littered the rocks. He dropped into the cockpit of his old wooden skiff and pulled the outboard cord. The well-maintained engine roared and within moments, Jay careened down the Warren River, headed for Narragansett Bay.

Brett calmly released the cinched webbing around the Zephyrus and picked up the forklift's remote control. He had a survey to complete before three o'clock.

Sabrina arrived at the boatyard a little early, anxious and excited to get started.

"Hi Mr. Story" she called out. The chubby man was bent under the hull, thumping it with a rubber mallet.

"Good afternoon, Miss Windham. I'm almost finished with the survey."

"What exactly is a survey?"

"Well, I examine the boat, the way a physician would a patient, looking for problems. I make a list and, based upon the survey, you know how much the boat is worth."

"I already know how much she's worth," Sabrina said. Her confidence had given her an aura of serenity. "Every penny."

"Must be nice to have money to burn, because that's what you're going to do with this clunker. Now, it breaks my heart as a businessman, but I should recommend that you forget restoring this boat. It's going to take at least six weeks of steady work and probably fifty thousand to make this boat new again. Well, new and improved."

"You don't want the job?" Sabrina cocked her head and smiled.

"Oh, believe me, I want the job. My boss, now, he's a different story." Brett sighed. He didn't want to do it, but Jay was too stubborn for his own good. "Can I talk to you openly?"

"Certainly."

"Let's go to Maude's. We're going to need a quiet booth and I'm going to need a beer."

"But it's only three o'clock," she protested.

"It's time," he said, matter-of-factly. He escorted her to the gate and locked the boatyard. In the distance, Sabrina heard muted barking of seals. The fence looked familiar, too. Uneasy, she looked over her shoulder. She opened her car door. "Shall I drive?"

"No; leave it. Maude's is just a couple of blocks away.

Let's go," he replied.

Sabrina felt déjà vu and shivered. "Maybe I need a beer, after all."

They walked quickly and soon she recognized the weathered tavern. The parking lot still contained motorcycles and pickup trucks. "Don't these people ever go home?"

Brett chuckled. "Yes, but they come back the next day."

Inside, the tavern looked friendly and its cedar-planked walls glowed in the filtered sunlight. Brett pointed to an empty booth near the back of the building. An old, stocky woman with frizzled gray hair approached them, menus and a dishtowel in her hands.

"Afternoon, Maude."

"Hey Brett. Where's Shawna today?" She eyed Sabrina with mistrust.

"She's at home, as always. This here is a client of the boatyard, Maude. She's picked up a sailboat that needs some work."

Maude nodded. "You mean that piece of crap you hauled by here this morning?"

Sabrina grimaced.

"Ayuh, that's the one," Brett said. "Miss Windham here has bought herself the original Zephyrus."

"Windham, you say?" Maude looked closely at Sabrina. "Don Windham's daughter? Nah, you're too young. You his kin?"

"Yes," Sabrina said, leaning forward eagerly. "You knew my grandfather?"

"Used to," Maude said, wiping the table and dropping the menus without ceremony. "Went to school with him and Derek. Those two were best friends. Tragedy that was, the fire."

Maude cleared her throat. "Listen, the kitchen isn't too busy if you two want something special."

"Thanks, Maude," Brett said. "Can we start with a

couple of lagers? Miss Windham, are you hungry?"

Rattled, Sabrina picked up the menu and scanned it. "Umm, actually, I am. I forgot to have lunch today. I'll have a bowl of chowder and a BLT."

Maude nodded. "Brett?"

"Thanks; I'll just have a beer. Shawna's cooking pot roast tonight," he said, rubbing his large belly.

Maude peered at him over her glasses. "You tell her I said hey, and good luck with the baby's teething."

Brett nodded and the old woman shambled off to the kitchen. He grinned at Sabrina. "She's a bit protective. Shawna's her grandniece."

"It's a small town, isn't it? It's amazing that she knew my grandfather. I never met him. He died a long time ago."

Brett nodded. "Yes, I know. In fact, that's what I need to talk to you about."

Curious, Sabrina leaned forward. "What is it?"

"Well, this could be a bit touchy. I mean, I don't know what happened last night when Jay left the bar after you, but …."

"Jay? What does this have to do with him?" Sabrina leaned back, frowning and blushing.

Brett nodded again, heaving a deep sigh. The woman was an open book.

"It's like this, Miss Windham, I like you, and I think you coming to Warren and finding this boat is something special. I mean it," he said, raising a hand when she tried to speak. "Don't stop me; I've got to get this out."

He paused long enough for Maude to plunk two frosty beers on the table. After she was out of earshot, he continued.

"I could tell something was happening last night. Jay never chases women, but he wouldn't take his eyes off you. The way he ran out of here. Well, I've never seen him act that way."

Sabrina bit her lip and looked away, unwilling to

comment.

"And I can see you got something going for him, too. Don't you?"

"Brett. If this is about my relationship with Jay, then you need to stop right now. I don't mean to be rude, but it's none of your business."

"See, that's the problem. It is my business," he said, gulping his beer. "Jay is my boss. He owns the boatyard."

She dropped her trembling hands into her lap. "That's bizarre," she said.

"Believe me; it's more bizarre than you think. Jay is the grandson of Derek West, your grandfather's partner."

"You're kidding me," she exclaimed. For the first time in her life, she understood the term "thunderstruck."

Brett nodded, satisfied that she understood, that she comprehended the uncanny situation.

"There's more. You see, Jay had a terrible childhood and his family, his grandmother, blame the Windhams for all their bad luck. He went berserk this morning when he saw the Zephyrus. He wanted to destroy it as soon as he laid eyes on it."

Sabrina's chin dropped and her eyes misted.

"When I told him who you are, pointed out that this is some kind of mystical connection, he got pissed off and left. Probably holed up in a bar downriver."

"I can't believe it. Oh, my God," she said, hiding her face in her shaky hands.

Maude returned, shoving a steaming bowl of chowder and a toasted BLT towards Sabrina.

"What's the matter?" She looked accusingly at Brett who silently mouthed "Jay," pointed to Sabrina's bowed head, then rolled his eyes. Maude grunted, and turned towards the kitchen, shaking her head. She owned a bar long enough to know love was a rocky road.

She stopped in her tracks, and turned slowly to look once more at Sabrina. A Windham and a West? Now she'd seen it all.

Long, silent moments passed. Brett drank his beer and regretted not ordering anything to eat. The chowder smelled tempting, and who could resist toast and bacon? After a few minutes, he began to squirm.

"Miss Windham. Eat your lunch."

She shook her head, still refusing to look up. Her heart ached and she felt on the verge of tears.

"Well," Brett said. "Do you mind if I eat the soup?"

That made her laugh and she sniffed, wiping her nose. She finally looked up and Brett saw sparkling tears in her eyes. She hiccupped, her breath hitching in her chest.

Oh, Grandmother Rose! She cringed at the memory of their talk.

"Mr. Story. It's awful. You don't know, nobody knows, what happened."

He spooned the creamy soup into his mouth and swallowed.

"You're wrong. Everybody knows," he said, nodding sagely.

CHAPTER EIGHT

It was late when Jay motored to the pier, tying the skiff to a cleat along the seawall. His head down, he strode to the back of the boatyard. The motion-detector light came on as he neared the steps to his apartment.

"I've been waiting for you."

He stumbled at the sound of the soft voice, then peered closely at the dark staircase. There, sitting on the second step, huddled in her long leather coat, was Sabrina.

"Go away," he muttered, searching his jeans for his house key.

Sabrina stood and leaned towards him, smelling smoke and bourbon.

"Are you drunk? She stepped closer, her hands in her coat pocket.

"Unfortunately, no. At least not very. You should leave," he said, refusing to look her in the eye. Instead, he concentrated on the boatyard light.

"I should," she whispered. "But I can't."

He frowned. All afternoon he had cursed her and her family, drowning his anger at a bayside bar. Now all he wanted to do was sink into her, inhale her musky perfume, taste her fevered lips. He looked away instead. Years of anger, years of hurt had hardened him.

Sabrina understood his rage. It wasn't simple for her to confront Jay, this intimate stranger, but she had to try to relieve his sorrow. "May I come upstairs? I'd like to speak with you," she said.

"I don't have anything to say to you."

"Well, may I come upstairs and not speak with you?"

The heat of his gaze stripped her and she burned for his hands to do the same.

"Kiss me," she whispered.

"Sabrina," he gasped, "I don't think ...."

"Good advice," she said, cutting off his words with her wicked mouth. She traced her tongue across his lips. "Let's not think about this."

* * *

Jay finished his sandwich, wadded the napkin and tossed it in the empty basket. "I needed that."

Brett spooned mashed potatoes and gravy into his mouth and groaned. "Ahh man, why can't Shawna cook like this? What's so hard about meatloaf?"

Jay shrugged. "Can't have it all, I guess."

Brett saw his opening. "Worked it out yet?"

"What?" Jay finished his root beer, stalling.

"You know damn well, 'what.' Are you going to work on the Zephyrus?"

Jay nodded.

"Well, that was easy," Brett teased. "What did she say to change your mind?"

Jay's eyelids drooped as he thought about Sabrina and her brash visit the night before. He couldn't deny the heat, the attraction between them, but that didn't mean he had to act upon it. After a head-spinning kiss, he'd put her aside, his hands firm on her shoulders.

"I'm not for sale," he said.

Sabrina cringed at his harsh tone. "I'm not trying to

buy you," she said. Moments passed in silence as she struggled between feelings of embarrassment, guilt and pity. "I like you," she said, hoping the childish statement explained all.

She hadn't said anything to him about the sailboat; hadn't tried to convince him to restore the Zephyrus. The cynic in him reminded him to be patient. She would.

Jay snorted, then realized he'd been holding his breath. He turned his back on Sabrina, trying to shut out the unexpected lightness he felt. His chest expanded as he inhaled. With each breath, he felt lighter. He could hear crickets and the murmur of seals along the sea wall. He heard Sabrina shuffle as she stepped off the stairs. Out of the corner of his eye, he saw her retreat to her car, shoulders slumped in defeat.

"I'll do it on one condition," he said.

Sabrina stopped in her tracks, then turned slowly, her hands fisted in her coat pocket. "Name it," she said, lifting her chin.

"The price is $200 per hour," he said.

Sabrina didn't flinch. In fact, she thought $200 was fair, if not cheap. "Fine," she said, stepping forward and holding out her hand.

"Not so fast," Jay said. "Two hundred per hour and sweat equity."

Sabrina was confused. "What is 'sweat equity'?"

Jay sneered. "You get your hands dirty, princess. You work on the boat, too."

Now it was Sabrina's turn to snort. "Are you joking? I don't know anything about boats."

"You will by the time we're finished."

Sabrina studied his tall frame, backlit by the boatyard light. They both stood still in the night, silently regarding each other. The motion detector turned off and they were plunged into darkness. Jay waved a hand and the brilliant light haloed him.

"Still interested?" he asked.

"Yes," Sabrina said with a frown. "We have a deal."

"Are you going to tell me what she said?" Brett's voice broke Jay's contemplation.

"It's not what she said. It's what I said. The fee is twice our normal rate, plus sweat equity."

Brett's mouth gaped. "You're going to make her work on the boat? In the shop?"

Jay squirmed on the hard, wooden stool. "Yeah."

"That's crazy," Brett said. "What about the liability? She doesn't have a clue about boats or probably even hard work."

"There's a lot of grunt work she can do," Jay replied, lifting his glass and rattling the ice. "Those are the terms. She agreed."

Brett heaved a huge sigh, then shook his head. "You got it bad, man. All this because you're hot for a rich girl."

"I'm not going to talk about her. You keep your fat mouth shut, too."

Brett raised his hands in surrender. "What'd I say?"

"Don't tell me you didn't spill your guts yesterday."

"You should be thanking me."

Jay shook his head in resignation. "I don't need help."

"What about Faye?" Brett prodded.

"What about her?"

"What are you going to do when she meets Sabrina Windham?"

"That won't happen."

"Are you kidding?"

"She's not going near her." Jay bristled. "She's not going to ruin this."

CHAPTER NINE

"Here, put these on," Brett said, handing Sabrina a pair of faded coveralls.

Gamely, she stepped into the faded, one-piece garment, then zipped it to her chin. The legs and arms drooped and for a moment, she felt like Dopey in the Disney cartoon. She held her arms out and grimaced.

"It fits fine," Brett assured her as he rolled up one sleeve. He rolled up the second sleeve and stepped back to assess. His chubby face broke into a grin. "Just hike up the legs and you'll be good to go."

They were alone in the shop. Jay had an early appointment at a nearby marina. A survey on a used boat in Newport would keep him away most of the day. He'd left strict orders for Brett to put Sabrina to work, scrubbing the Zephyrus, inside and out.

Sabrina was relieved. She still felt embarrassed that she'd tracked down Jay the night before, ambushing him on the stairs and kissing him senseless, only to be rejected. She'd arrived on time, armed with pride, only to be mollified by Brett's humor and welcoming nature. After a short tour of the workshop, which included coffee and donuts, she and Brett were fast friends on a first-name basis.

The workshop was cavernous, with a two-story main building and two bays. The massive double doors stood open and each time the occasional car drove past, Sabrina watched, anxious for Jay's return. She wanted to see him again, even though the thought tied her stomach in knots.

She surveyed the shop, noting the interior staircase that lead to Jay's apartment. Her cheeks heated as she recalled her visit there and the passionate kisses they shared. She'd tossed and turned the night before, remembering his hands and his lips and the frustration she'd felt at his rejection.

She turned her attention back to the shop. The interior was uninsulated, bare plywood. Several workbenches spanned the walls and the floor was littered with wood shavings. A half-built wooden hull dominated the middle of the shop.

In one bay of the large, messy shop, the Zephyrus balanced between boat stands. Without its keel, it looked like a beached whale. It looked larger than she remembered, perched on the blue steel posts.

Sabrina relaxed as Brett explained her task for the day. "Shoot, I've cleaned worse messes," she bragged. "This is nothing."

But, as the morning wore on, her arms began to ache from hauling buckets of soapy water and holding the scrub brush over her head. Looking around the shop, she spied a pair of unused sawhorses. She dragged them to the side of the boat, then wrangled several long boards atop. She placed a five-gallon bucket next to her homemade scaffold, then climbed atop. When she finished the starboard hull, she moved her scaffold to the port side. Soon, the chalky white hull was clean and Sabrina knew every dent, every crack, including a new one on the bow. She slipped her fingers into the fresh crack, her water-wrinkled fingertips caressing the fibers and brittle resin.

"Let's break for lunch," Brett said. When she turned, she noticed Brett frowning at the crack in the bow. "Jay did that yesterday," he explained. "I thought he was going to destroy her. He's got a lot of anger inside him."

Sabrina looked at the boat and chewed her lip. "Do you think I should leave? Maybe take the Zephyrus somewhere else?"

Brett shook his head. "No, not at all. It's crazy, you being here and finding her, but it's kinda cool. There's got to be something meaningful about this. I'm not a hippy, or anything like that, but it's more than a coincidence."

"It's serendipitous?" Sabrina offered.

"Yeah, whatever that means. Come on, let's go to Maude's. I'm starved."

* * *

Sabrina studied the menu. "I'll have the Cobb Salad and the soup of the day," she told Maude. "And a cup of hot tea, please."

Maude turned her attention to Brett. "This gonna be a regular thing?" she asked, tilting her head towards Sabrina.

Brett kept his eyes on his menu, as if he needed one. "Miss Windham is working on her boat this week," he said. "I'll take a meatball hoagie, chips and a beer."

Maude waited until Brett looked her way, then gave him the evil eye. "You'll take a salad, too. No chips and no beer. Diet soda. Chowder, okay for the both of you?"

At their mutual nods, Maude shuffled off to the kitchen. Brett heaved a sigh. "I'm guess I'm going to have invite you to dinner tonight, to meet the Missus."

"You don't have to do that," Sabrina said, giggling at his reluctant tone.

"No, Shawna needs to meet you and give her seal of approval. If she doesn't, Maude's going to keep punishing me with healthy food," Brett said, pulling out his cell phone. He dialed home and Sabrina excused herself while he spoke to his wife.

She pushed open the door to the restroom and entered

the gloomy, but clean single stall. The soap dispenser emitted a gray grit and she washed her hands in the old-fashioned, two-spigot sink, alternating between the cold and too-hot water. The mirror above the sink had lost most of its silvering, but she could still tell her hair was a mess and she had a streak of white chalk on her cheek. She used a rough, brown paper towel to scrub her face. She'd left her purse at the table, so she finger-combed her dark hair until it lay flat.

As she walked out of the restroom, Maude slid two steaming bowls of clam chowder onto to the bar. Then she slapped cloth napkins and spoons on the wood surface. "Here you go," she said to Sabrina.

Sabrina lifted an empty tray from the end of the counter, placed the cutlery and bowls on it. "Thanks," she said, grinning at the gruff, old woman. Maude nodded, a reluctant smile crinkling her saggy cheeks.

When Sabrina arrived at the table, Brett handed her the cell phone. "She wants to talk to you."

Sabrina held the phone to her ear. "Hello?"

A girlish voice swamped her senses. "Well, hello yourself. I'm Shawna Story and Brett has told me so much about you. I can't wait to meet you. We're having lasagna tonight. Is that okay with you? If not, I can change the menu."

"Hello Shawna," Sabrina said. "No, no, lasagna is fine. I love Italian food. I'm looking forward to meeting you, as well."

The bubbly voice continued. "We'll have dinner at six so make sure that Brett doesn't work you to death today. I heard how you're slaving away at the boatyard. That Jay West is a pisser. I'm going to have to give him a piece of my mind."

Hearing his wife's voice grow shrill, Brett held out his hand for the phone.

"Thank you again, Shawna, for the invitation. Brett would like to speak with you," Sabrina said, passing him the phone in gratitude.

"Okay, Babe, we'll see you tonight. And would you please call off your Great-Aunt Maude? I really would like a hoagie." Brett punched the off button and placed the mobile on the table. He looked around expectantly. The bar phone rang and Maude shuffled from the kitchen to answer it. A minute later, she hung up and glared at Brett. The couple pretended to watch the television until she banged her way back into the kitchen.

"You really didn't have to invite me to dinner," Sabrina said.

"Oh yes I did. Shawna is curious about you, and Maude is protective. It doesn't matter that you're Jay's ..."

"I am not Jay's!" Sabrina interrupted. "I am not a piece of property and I don't belong to anyone."

Brett eyed her warily. "Okay," he drawled. "Guess I shouldn't have said that. What I meant was, you and Jay seem awfully interested in each other."

Sabrina pouted. "Maybe. But that was before he knew my background. I'm a Windham. I'm the enemy."

"You know what they say. Keep your enemy close," Brett misquoted.

"'Keep your friends close, but your enemies closer.' Godfather, Part Two," Sabrina corrected him.

Maude slammed trays onto the bar counter. "Foods up!"

Brett sprang from his chair to pick up the trays. Instead of a hoagie, Maude had dumped meatballs and melted cheese atop a salad. He shrugged. "Thanks, Maude. I love you!"

* * *

After scrubbing the cockpit and bailing more fetid water from the Zephyrus, Sabrina stepped into the small salon. Hearing a faint rustle, she approached the galley warily. She lifted a moldy towel and spied straw in the sink.

Several soft, yellow chicks peeped at her from the nest.

"Oh, you darlings," she crooned. She thought she'd removed all the chickens before the boat had been moved, but she missed this one. The eggs must have hatched during the night. She reached out a timid finger and touched the downy feathers. The chicks chirped and huddled around her hand, seeking warmth.

"What am I going to do with you? Darn you, Mr. Blair!" she cooed and cursed.

"Who are you talking to?"

Sabrina froze at the sound of Jay's gruff voice outside the boat. Seconds later, she heard him on the scaffold. The boat rocked as he climbed aboard. "Careful!" she cried out.

"It's fine," he assured her as he swung into the cabin. "What do you have there?"

Sabrina couldn't see his face in the gloom, but he could see hers, as it wreathed in a smile.

"Baby chickens." She picked up one of the peeps, her hand gentle under its feather weight. She brushed it against her cheek. "They're so cute!"

A smile curled the corner of Jay's mouth. "Where's the mama?"

"She must be at Mr. Blair's farm. The man who sold me the boat," she explained. "I suppose we need to return them."

Jay leaned against the keel-stepped mast pole and crossed his arms. "Unless you're going to start raising chickens, too."

He took a moment to study the boat's interior. "I have to say; you're going to need a lot of sweat equity to square this boat away. It's a piece of junk."

"It is not a piece of junk!" Sabrina placed the chick back in its nest. "Will you please get me a bucket? I need to move the chicks out of here so I can continue cleaning."

Jay pushed off the post and climbed the steps to the

cockpit. "Get it yourself, Princess" he tossed over his shoulder.

Sabrina glared at his back. "Fine! I will. And quit calling me Princess," she retorted.

By the time she clambered topside, Jay was across the shop and climbing the inner stairs to his apartment. He didn't look back. She stuck her tongue out and then noticed Brett.

"Is he always belligerent? Or, is it just me?"

"Well, he's a bit prickly, but I'm thinking you bring out the worst in him," Brett said. "Give him some time. He'll get over it."

Sabrina dropped the chicks off at the Blair farm before heading to her hotel. She'd scrubbed and cleaned the Zephyrus until five o'clock, and her arms and back were aching from the effort. The harsh chemicals used in cleaning the boat left her hands blistered and cracking. She was tired and running out of clean clothes. She hadn't packed for manual labor.

She asked at the front desk about a shopping mall, only to learn the closest was twenty minutes away. She wouldn't be able to squeeze in a trip before dinner with the Storys. Her hope was to eat and run and pray the hosts weren't insulted.

After a short soak in the hotel tub, she showered and shaved, then pampered her skin with her favorite brand of organic, vanilla-scented lotion. She dressed in her cleanest dirty clothes, a button-down shirt and jeans. She had a few minutes to spare, so she dialed her grandmother's hospital room. Shirley Piper answered on the second ring, then passed the phone to Rose.

"Hello Darling," Rose whispered.

"Well, Grandmother, you're not going to believe this, but I've met Jay West."

Sabrina heard a gasp on the end of the line. Seconds

passed in silence. "Grandmother, are you there?"

"Jay West? As in, the West family?"

"Yes; he's the son of Margaret West. Not only that, he owns the boatyard where I have the Zephyrus."

"What?"

"I met him my first night in town, but I didn't know who he was. We kind of, um, made out. Then, when I found out who he was, it was too late."

"Made out? Too late? As in …"

"No, not that. Too late as in the Zephyrus was at his boatyard."

"My goodness. Well, what next?"

"I'm not sure. I've finally convinced him to restore the boat."

"I thought you said they picked up the boat. Didn't you give him a deposit?"

"I gave the deposit to his assistant manager, Brett Story. He's the one I talked to on the telephone, and he picked up the boat. I had no idea Jay was involved until after the boat was delivered. Brett told me that Jay was furious when he saw the Zephyrus. He wanted to destroy it."

"Why would he want to do that?"

"Brett told me that Jay's mother was an alcoholic and took drugs, and that she died of an overdose when he was twelve."

"How tragic!"

"He went to live with his grandmother, who apparently had gone off the deep end. She poisoned him with stories of the Windhams. About how you ruined her life. He left home for a while, went to college in Maine and studied naval architecture. When he returned, he started the boatyard."

"And now the Zephyrus is at his boatyard?" Rose said.

"Yes, and not only that, I have to pay what he calls 'sweat equity.' I must work on the boat, too. I spent all day washing and scrubbing the hull."

Rose sighed. "Sabrina, do you believe in destiny?"

"I'm beginning to."

Dinner at Brett and Shawna's house was more complicated than Sabrina imagined. Unbeknownst to her, Shawna had invited Jay West. He was already seated at the table when she arrived. A six-month old cherub sat in a high chair next to Brett. Shawna busted around the kitchen, setting a salad on the table, followed by a steaming casserole dish of fragrant lasagna.

Sabrina sat across the table from Jay, avoiding eye contact while Brett spooned pureed carrots into the baby's mouth. Throughout the meal, Shawna chatted about Warren, their new baby and her scrapbooking club, trying to find a common, neutral topic.

"Excuse me, I'm sorry, what did you say?" Sabrina asked.

Shawna exchanged a quick look with Brett. "I asked if you collect snapshots. Family memorabilia and such. If so, I'd be happy to show you how to put them in a scrapbook."

Sabrina shook her head. "Um, thanks so much, but I don't. I'm an only child and my parents travel quite a bit. They're writers, so they document their trips. If I want to know what they're up to, I order their latest book from Amazon or turn on the travel channel."

Shawna's mouth gaped. Brett's hand paused in mid-motion. Even Jay was startled into looking her in the eye.

"You mean, you don't talk to your own parents?" Shawna asked in disbelief.

Sabrina bit her lip. "I'm sorry, I didn't mean to give the wrong impression. We speak. They're just nomads, in their own little world. They always have been."

Jay frowned. "You went to boarding school," he recalled from a previous conversation. "You're an only child? Like me."

"It sounds rather pathetic when you say it like that," she said, her smile forlorn. "But you're right. We're both the last little branches on our family's trees."

Shawna saw her opening. "I think it's just amazing that you found your way here and that you've found each other."

Brett frowned and shook his head in warning.

Ever gracious, Sabrina overlooked the woman's attempt to match make. "Our families have an interesting history, but it isn't that unusual. This is where the Zephyrus was built. What's amazing is the first one still exists."

"Barely," Jay growled. "It's not worth the effort or the money. You'd be better off without it. It's a piece of …"

"I know what you think it is," Sabrina said, interrupting him. "But it's my time and it's my money. I think it's worth it. The Zephyrus is more than a boat."

She turned her attention to Shawna. "It's a way for me to connect with my family and their history. Even if it's a tragic history."

"Tragic? You don't know the meaning of the word," Jay said, his voice breaking with bitterness. He pushed himself away from the table. "I've got to go."

He stood and strode to the front door. He paused, remembering his manners, and thanked Shawna. "It was a great dinner. Thanks again."

They sat in silence as the door slammed behind him. Moments later, Sabrina put her napkin on the table. "I'm sorry, but I should be going, also."

Shawna walked her to the door and gave her a brief hug. "You need to be patient with him," she whispered, looking over her shoulder at her befuddled husband. "Maybe you should try to talk to him?"

Sabrina shook her head. "No, that's not a good idea. Besides, I need to get to the mall and pick up some work clothes. I've got a long week ahead of me."

CHAPTER TEN

B ut somehow, she ended up at Jay's apartment. She meant to drive to the mall. She really did, but at the last minute she whipped the Cadillac into the boatyard and marched to the backstairs.

He sat on the bottom step, his face in his hands. He looked up at her approach.

"We have to stop meeting this way," he said.

All the angry words she'd practiced in the car were forgotten. The only thing that mattered was the misery she saw etched in his face.

"I want to apologize," she said. "I know we have such different backgrounds. Yes, I've had privilege and a loving family. Well, a loving grandmother, at least." She laughed awkwardly. "I mean, I know my parents love me. They gave me everything my heart desired."

Jay said nothing.

"I'm not doing this very well," she continued. "What I mean is, I know you've suffered and your family suffered, and it's my family's fault, but can't you try to forgive me for their sins?"

Jay stood, towering over her. Sabrina flinched, but held her ground.

"Do you want a drink?" he asked.

Nonplussed, Sabrina stammered, "Okay."

She followed him up the stairs and into the dark loft. She dropped her purse and keys by the door, shutting it behind her.

Jay pulled a bottle of Tequila from beneath his bar, then slumped on the dark blue sofa. He pulled the cork from the bottle and upended it, gulping as the amber liquid slid down his throat. He handed her the bottle.

"Um, thanks? I'm going to get us a couple of glasses," she said. She put the bottle on the side table and went behind the bar. She opened cabinet doors until she found clean glasses.

She poured two fingers for herself, then for Jay. She handed him the glass and held hers out in a toast. "Friends?"

Jay took the glass and drank it without toasting. Then took her glass from her trembling fingers and put it on the table.

He pulled her into his arms, cupping her head against his chest.

Sabrina froze, unsure what to make of his gentle embrace. Seconds passed, then she lifted her chin. Jay's hand slipped from the back of her head to cup her cheek. His mouth captured hers and she tasted tequila. She wrapped her arms around his neck and sank into the cushions, pulling him against her.

His drugging kiss invited her to open her mouth and she whimpered at the sensation of his tongue stroking hers. She needed more. She needed to feel his skin against hers. She slid her hands inside his T-shirt.

"Honey, we need to slow down," he said, pulling back.

"I don't want to. If I do, I might change my mind." She sat up and tugged at her shirt, pulling the buttons loose and shimmying free.

She rose on her knees and pressed him into the back of the couch, hypnotizing him with one deep kiss after another. While Sabrina focused on tugging off his T-shirt, Jay slipped his hands behind her and unsnapped her red and black satin bra. As the wisp of material fell away, he marveled at the dark peaks of her breasts. Her skin was dusky and smelled faintly of cinnamon and, he inhaled again, hay?

Unable to resist, he brushed his tongue against her nipple. She reacted instantly, arching her back and thrusting her breasts forward. Jay placed a hand over one swollen nipple, rolling it gently between his fingers, while he tugged the other between his lips. His free hand slid down her waist and cupped her bottom. Sabrina straddled Jay, resting on her knees. When she felt the pressure of his hand on the back of her thigh, she lowered herself into his lap and rocked gently.

"Hold on," Jay cautioned. "Not here. You're going too fast."

"I know," she murmured, "I'm burning up." She nuzzled against his beard, rubbing it first with her cheek, then her shoulder. Moaning softly, she captured his face turning his mouth to hers. Between each intoxicating kiss, she gasped for air.

"This is so strange," she whispered, her heated breath misting his ear, "but I need you." Her voice was husky, strangled with tears. "Now!"

Pulling her to her feet, he led Sabrina into the next room, to his unmade bed with its inviting, cool sheets.

"First, let's take care of these," he said, brushing his lips against her neck. Reaching for her waistband, he tugged her against him and slid the zipper down its track. He cupped her hips and pushed her jeans to the floor.

Sabrina stepped out of them, wearing only her panties and a pair of white crew socks. Without doubt, she was the most exquisite woman Jay had ever seen, much less touched.

She moved into his embrace and he concentrated on kissing her, caressing her silky back. Sabrina deftly unsnapped buttons and his jeans followed hers to the floor. Her fingers slid beneath the band of his boxers. "These too," she murmured against his chest.

Within moments, they were wrapped in each other's arms and rolling on the bed. Sabrina felt charged, electricity sparking from her fingers as she touched his body. She luxuriated in the taste of him as her silky, agile tongue danced across his skin. She whispered in his ear, words outrageously exciting and sensual.

The roughness of his worker's hands lightly teased her nipples to aching hardness. Every inch of her skin tingled as he stroked her belly, her thighs, the small of her back, the inside of her elbows.

His skin next to hers seared, and she could not touch him enough. The soft, dark hair on his chest tickled her fingers, and she thrilled at the solid, flat planes of his back. His lips touched a nipple, tenderly at first, then insatiably. He suckled with a delicate strength that made her gasp and bow her back.

With her legs wrapped around him, sliding and shifting under him, she bucked restlessly and begged for release. It was tearing her apart, this throbbing need that only he could satisfy.

When he slid his fingers between them, he found her swollen and damp. "Ahh, Sabrina," he groaned and kissed her again.

He trembled, his eyes closed as if in prayer, when Sabrina slipped her hand around him, holding and exploring him with audacious curiosity. She could wait no longer. She fitted him between her thighs.

Lowering his lips into to the fragrant hollow of her neck, he drove into her with measured force. He grasped her wrists and pulled them above her head. With her pinned and him sliding in and out with a steady rhythm, he noticed that he hadn't removed her panties. The friction of the lacy band drove him wild, and his control slipped.

Sabrina wanted to claw at him, yank his hair, and

scream her need. With every thrust, she felt his wildness and despaired that she would not find release in time. Then, as he closed his mouth on her breast, it happened. He buried himself inside her, hard and hot, thick and smooth, and she spiraled over the edge. He liberated her hands and held her close, urging her, and it was stronger and sweeter than anything she experienced before.

As she fluttered downward, her body spent and weak, he tensed. Then, with a rough cry of fulfillment, he collapsed against her. She could feel him tremble as he rolled over. She pillowed her head on his chest and closed her eyes.

It was dark. Sabrina lay curled against Jay, his possessive arm tossed over her hips. His breathing was deep, his chest rising and falling in a steady rhythm. She eased herself away, sliding toward the edge of the bed. When she made it, she stood in the moonlight and watched him sleep.

"Uh oh, Grandmother. Now I know what happened to you," she whispered, her eyes tender as she watched him sleep.

Sabrina gritted her teeth, and then searched the shadowy floor for her scattered clothes. She tiptoed into the living room where she dressed in a hurry, pulling her wrinkled shirt from between the couch cushions. She laced her shoes and wiggled into her coat. She knew her makeup and hair were a mess, but she had to get out of there now, before he woke and she had to look into his eyes.

Six years of Catholic school training were not a complete waste. Shame flushed her cheeks. She opened the door as quietly as possible and let herself out into the night. It closed with an audible click, but Jay was sound asleep. Sabrina raced down the steps, cringing when her footsteps alerted a seal and it barked hoarsely.

She sprinted to the middle of the dark street and after

looking both ways saw the illuminated hotel sign in the distance. Once in the Cadillac, she opened her purse and withdrew a brush. With wild, frantic yanks, she smoothed her hair. She tucked her shirt into her jeans and buttoned her jacket. She searched her purse for the hotel key card and panicked. Then, with a sigh of relief, she found it in her back pocket. The last thing she wanted to do was ask the hotel clerk for another key; especially at, what time was it? She pulled out her cell phone and pushed a button. The screen lit up: 12:48 a.m.

She drove the short distance to the hotel and parked. With her head averted, she let herself into the hotel lobby and walked towards the stairs to her second-floor suite. The clerk looked up from his magazine briefly and then ignored her.

In her room at last, Sabrina leaned against the door and giggled. She stepped into the bathroom, the light and fan driving away the quiet. She turned on the shower and began to strip. She yelped softly when she saw red marks on her breasts and belly, and licked her swollen, aching lips.

"Mmmmm!" She wrapped her arms around her shoulders and giggled again. Then, hefting her tender breasts in each hand, she examined them for small hickeys. She raised an eyebrow at her reflection. "You should see the other guy," she quipped.

Soon, the steaming shower, fragrant soap and soothing body lotion dispelled her aches, leaving her skin glowing and soft. Later, lying naked in her bed, she ran her hands over her belly and between her thighs. She squeezed her eyes and regretted leaving him, yearning again for his touch, his kiss, his powerful body against hers.

Then she slept, hugging her pillow.

CHAPTER ELEVEN

The next morning, Sabrina showed up for work before Jay. Brett had the double doors open, the radio playing.

"Good morning," he said. 'There's a box of donuts on the workbench. Coffee is still brewing. Help yourself."

A donut clenched between her teeth, she stepped into the dirty coveralls and wrinkled her nose. She needed to get the mall today. New clothes and clean clothes were no longer an option.

She poured a cup of steaming coffee next and turned towards Brett. "What's on the agenda for today, boss?"

Brett arched a brow. Sabrina looked perky and rested. "Have to say, I'm glad you're back. I figured yesterday's chores would have you hightailing home."

Sabrina smiled. "I'm tougher than you think. If I can graduate from Harvard with honors, I can scrub a boat."

With his foot, he pushed a bucket her way. Inside were rolls of sandpaper and small blocks of wood. "Today, you sand the teak. We need her down to bare wood."

She picked up a faded ball cap and put it on her head, flicking her ponytail through the clasp. Her coffee in one hand, she picked up the bucket handle with the other.

"Can do."

Thirty minutes later, Jay appeared, freshly showered and smelling like heaven as he bent over Sabrina. "What are you doing?" he asked. "Who showed you how to sand teak?"

Sabrina looked up, leaning against his legs. "Nobody. Do you like it?"

Jay shook his head. "It's got to be done all over. You need to sand with the grain, honey, not against it. Look, this is how you do it." He picked up a fresh sheet of sandpaper, wrapped it around a block of wood, and briskly rubbed it in the opposite direction. "See, with the grain. Then you don't get all these cross hatches."

In the far bay, Brett watched the interplay. He didn't miss the fact that Jay had called her "honey" or that he had his large hand wrapped around hers, rubbing the teak with easy, expert strokes. He saw Sabrina's cheeks turn rosy and her eyes brighten. Any fool could see the tension between them had eased.

"Why did you leave? I missed you this morning," Jay said in a low voice, his hand dropping the sand block and moving to her hip.

Sabrina swatted his hand away. "I had to be at work bright and early. I made a deal and I always keep my word," she teased.

Before Jay could respond, the phone rang.

"Hey Jay, can you get that? I'm mixing epoxy over here," Brett called out.

He swiveled off the side of the boat. His construction boots made a loud slap as he landed in a pile of wood shavings. The phone call stretched into a drawn-out, heated conversation. Sabrina watched furtively as Jay began to pace. The person on the other end of the call was relentless, and even though she couldn't make his words, she could tell Jay resented the interrogation. She wondered who could agitate him so quickly and why he didn't hang up. A niggling feeling in her stomach told her it was another woman. Someone he cared about.

When he finally hung up, he looked in her direction. Sabrina pretended not to notice as she sanded the stained and weather-beaten wood. When she glanced up again, he was gone.

She heard the roar of a pickup truck and tires spinning in the gravel. Curiosity overcame her and she decided she needed a break and a little conversation.

"Can I fix you a cup of coffee?" she called to Brett. She took his thumbs up as a "yes" and took him coffee and the box of donuts. She flipped an empty bucket and sat on it, watching as Brett spread epoxy onto two boards, then clamp them together. "Making a new tiller," he said by way of explanation."

Sabrina nodded as if she understood, then cut to the chase. "Where did Jay go?"

Brett stretched, took a quaff of his coffee and bit into a donut. "Mmm, that's good."

"Quit stalling and spill," she commanded.

Brett shuffled his feet. "To Faye's," he said, then quickly amended, "Faye is his grandmother."

"He seemed distressed," Sabrina said, a frown creasing her brow.

"Faye's a bit demanding."

Sabrina relented. "I'm sorry, I shouldn't be pestering you about his private life. You're his best friend." She put her cup on the bench and stood. "Well, back to work. I want to get some progress made by lunchtime. I need to head out a little early today. Go to the mall and pick up some items."

Brett nodded. Women sure went into detail. Shawna was the same. No unspoken thoughts.

He and Jay usually worked in companionable silence with various projects going at the same time. They staggered chores, varnishing teak, then repairing engines while the woodwork dried. They seldom needed conversation, and when they did talk it was never boring.

Jay missed Sabrina by ten minutes.

"The mall? What does she need at the mall?" he asked.

Brett shrugged his shoulders. "I don't know, man. She said she needed some new clothes."

Jay rolled his eyes and got to work installing an autopilot on a new sloop.

At five o'clock, Brett turned off the radio. "Beer at Maude's?"

"Sure," Jay said, wiping his hands on a rag. He shoved the red flannel into his back pocket. "Why don't you head over? I'll be along shortly."

"Sure. Want me to order you anything?"

"Yeah, I'll take a hoagie, no onions."

After Brett left, Jay walked over to the Zephyrus. He touched the crack he made in the gel coat. He ran his hand along the hull, stroking the swollen belly above the waterline. He closed his eyes and tried to imagine how Derek West must have felt when the finished boat came out of the shop. Did he feel pride in his workmanship?

As a student, he had studied naval design, including the Zephyrus. Now, he looked beyond the dull finish, the pitted propeller, the broken keel, and chipped rudder. He closed his eyes and leaned against the boat, waiting for it to speak to him, a silent communion.

In his mind's eye, he could see her as she once had been, with foamy waves splashing against the gleaming white hull as she slid across the deep blue Massachusetts Bay. The sleek double-ender sailboat with its salty cabin and proud bow designed by Don Windham and built by Derek West had been a classic beauty.

She will be again, he vowed.

CHAPTER TWELVE

The rest of the week continued as it began — with Jay and Sabrina running hot and cold. By day, they worked in the boatyard, Jay rewiring the sloop, and Sabrina doing grunt work on the Zephyrus.

She joined Jay and Brett for lunch at Maude's most days.

At night, she joined Jay in his loft apartment, but not without keeping him waiting.

The second night she joined him, it was after nine o'clock and he'd been wondering if she would show. He spent two long hours at Maude's nursing one beer after another. When Shawna called, demanding he return her husband, he headed home.

Sabrina met him at the back stairs, then, she let her long, leather coat fall open. Beneath it, she wore only a bra and panties.

With a growl, Jay crushed her against his chest and his mouth ravaged hers. Sabrina encircled his neck with her arms, melting into him, yielding to his fury. He released her long enough to pull her up the stairs. He fumbled with the key, unlocked the door clumsily. Inside, he slammed it shut and shoved her against it.

In the dark, against the wood barrier, he devastated her with his kiss, punished her with his sensual mouth. Unwilling to release her, he shoved her panties down with one hand and stroked her, sliding fingers into the wetness. With sharp teeth, he tugged at her bra until her breasts were free, then he sucked voraciously on hardened nipples. Sabrina panted and squirmed against his questing touch. She arched her back, begging him to suckle one breast, then the other. She whimpered when he removed his fingers, then sighed when it was replaced with his long, hot, hard shaft. She wiggled her hips, slipping and sliding around him as he pushed against her velvety softness.

He cupped her bottom, lifting her feet off the floor, pinning her. He buried his face in her soft, dark hair and, audacious and urgent, his hands slid her up and down his length. Suspended between the wall and his body, straining closer, needing him deeper, she wrapped her legs around his waist.

The soft sounds coming from deep in her throat and the impatient touch of her hands assured him that despite his ferocity, he pleased her. He rested against her for a moment, trembling and fighting for control. She wouldn't allow it, biting at his shoulder and plunging her tongue into his ear.

"Wait; don't move," he whispered against her neck.

"I can't help it," she moaned, shifting fluidly with an intuitive pace. The slow, swirl of her hips drove him insane and with a roar, he picked up his own rhythm. She cried out when she felt the crest and rode each wave of ecstasy. As she quivered with the joy that only he could provide she felt him plunge one final time. Then, they both sagged. In the dark, she listened to his labored breathing and felt him tremble as he held her.

Nestled in the sheets of his bed, Sabrina slept. As the sky lightened, Jay watched her sleep, savoring the fine bones of her face, the soft curve of her neck. Exotic, with long lashes and dark, rich hair, she didn't look like a Windham. He had seen photos of both Don and Rose, yet he couldn't see either of them in Sabrina.

Sabrina stretched, opening her eyes slowly. When she saw him, she smiled, her lush, swollen lips parting. She scooted into the curve of his body and sighed. She traced his jaw, tickling his beard and lips. She rubbed a finger in the crease between his eyebrows.

"Don't frown."

Jay closed his eyes slowly.

"Maybe this is the way it's supposed to be," she whispered against his neck.

"Now you sound like Brett."

"Maybe he's right."

"What did he tell you?" Jay rolled onto his back.

"Nothing I didn't already know," Sabrina said, laying her head on his chest. She listened to the sound of his heart, heard it speed up as his anxiety mounted.

"You knew? From the beginning, you knew?"

"I knew about our grandparents. I didn't know you existed. Didn't know who you were when we met. When we first kissed …" she faltered. "I didn't know the connection until the next day when Brett told me."

"What the hell does he know?" Jay slid a hand up her naked back.

"Well," she said, snuggling into his embrace, "he says he knows 'everything,' whatever that means. That everyone knows. Does that mean the whole town?"

Jay nodded. "Yeah, I'm afraid it does. My grandmother went nuts. She made sure that everybody knew Rose Windham was an adulterer. She blamed the fire on Rose. Said she killed them."

"It's true," Sabrina said, sighing. "Rose told me about it after I found some letters and a newspaper clipping. It was horrible. So tragic."

"You don't look anything like her, do you?"

"No. I look like my mother. She's Brazilian. She and my father met in college."

"She must be very beautiful," he said, stroking her cheek.

Sabrina turned her head and kissed his palm. "When I first saw you, I thought you were scary. Dark and brooding and dangerous."

"But not anymore?"

"No. I guess I've developed a taste for danger. And all these hard muscles," she said, squeezing his arm.

"I've been too rough with you," he said, contrite. "I've hurt you, haven't I?"

He held her against the pillows and studied her, noting the red marks, the swollen lips. "What have I done to you?"

Sabrina chuckled and cuddled him to her breasts. "Don't be silly. I'm not made of glass. You haven't done anything that I haven't wanted. Or haven't done to you."

"No, it's not right. A man doesn't hurt a woman."

"I'm fine," she said. "Look, if you're going to be a crybaby every time we have sex …," she teased.

"You want a 'tough guy' to have sex with, is that it?" He took advantage of his position and rubbed his beard against her hardening nipples.

"Well, I've never had one before and it is kind of fun," she reasoned, arching an eyebrow.

"Posh girl comes to town, trolling for trouble."

"No, girl comes to town to find boat. I don't troll for men," she said, stiffening. "Does it really bother you? The money?"

"Sabrina, it's never a problem for those who have it."

She pushed him away. "Maybe I better go." She lifted gracefully from the bed and sorted through clothing and sheets, looking for her underwear.

He rolled on his back and watched her with distrust. "They're in the living room," he offered.

She glared at him, then stomped into the other room.

100

She returned a minute later, clad in her bra and panties, her coat slung over her arm. "What is the matter with you? Why do you want to pick a fight?"

When he didn't answer, she dropped her coat and slithered up the bed, crawling on her hands and knees until she covered him. Straddling him, she picked up his hands and placed them on her hips. Slowly she moved against him. "Is this the only way we can get along?"

She lowered herself until her lips were an inch from his. "Make love, not war," she murmured, then gently kissed him.

He proceeded to do just that: caressing her weary body, whispering endearments against the soft skin of her neck. His deep, drugging kisses put her in a stupor. For the next hour, he made love to her with an aching tenderness, caressing her until her soft sighs became breathless pants.

Sabrina felt adored as he held her, stroking and kissing her to sweet abandon. She saw the sun's glow reflected in his eyes and moaned his name softly, before his mouth covered hers again. She wanted this, and more. Maybe this wild, sexual attraction could be love, she thought, then he entered her with slow deliberateness and she stopped thinking.

His steady, measured strokes set the rhythm and despite her attempts to quicken the pace, he controlled their lovemaking. Tension built and Sabrina clung to him, begging for release, covering his neck and chest with frantic kisses until a quaking rush tore through her.

He feels it too, she thought, as they floated to earth, their mouths fused, their trembling arms wrapped around each other. Will he tell me? She wondered.

With supreme effort, Sabrina opened her eyes. Jay's insistent alarm clock buzzed. She pulled a pillow over her head as he reached for the off button. She felt the bed sag as he sat up, heard his feet thump against the floor.

She lifted the pillow. "Lover boy …," she began in a soft, wheedling voice.

Jay looked amused. "Yes?"

"Will you get my bag of clothes?"

"Where is it?"

She stretched luxuriously. "Mmmm. It's in my car," she said, exhaling deeply. She licked her swollen lips then burrowed into his pillow and closed her eyes.

She reminded Jay of a contented cat and he stroked her rounded bottom. She sighed again and mumbled something unintelligible.

"What?" he asked, leaning down.

"Sabes que eu te amo," she whispered, her eyes closed, her breathing deep. She was on the verge of sleep.

"I don't understand. What did you say?"

When Sabrina didn't answer, Jay shrugged and pulled on a pair of jeans. He went into the great room, making coffee at the kitchenette. Lifting one of his sail curtains, he saw Sabrina's massive Cadillac parked on the street next to the boatyard's padlocked front gate.

As the coffee brewed, Jay padded down the steps to the boatyard. He hadn't bothered with shoes, and the dew was cold against his bare feet. When he reached the Cadillac, he saw that she had left it unlocked, but she also had left the keys in ignition. Just in case she needed a quick getaway, he mused. On the passenger seat was her purse and a small bag he imagined contained clothes. He slid in, turned the key, and the massive engine purred to life. Shifting it into drive, he steered the car down to the alley, to the back of the boatyard where his own pickup truck rested. He parked it, collected her bags and exited the car, tucking her keys in his jeans pocket.

As he made his way to the stairs, he heard tires crunching on gravel. Brett maneuvered his truck into the empty space beside Sabrina's car. Catching sight of Jay, he wolf-whistled through the open window.

Jay grinned, barefoot and bare-chested on the stairs,

and lifted Sabrina's purse and bag as way of explanation.

Brett nodded. "Guess you're going to be late again," he joked. "Man. Must be nice to be the boss." He chuckled, watching Jay bound up the steps.

Back upstairs, Jay deposited Sabrina's purse and bag at the foot of the bed. He took a cup of steaming coffee into the shower with him, and in fifteen minutes was dressed and ready for work.

He knelt at the bed and stroked Sabrina's glossy hair.

"Wake up, honey," he urged.

Sabrina stirred, opening her eyes. Confused at first, when she recognized him, they softened.

Jay's heart sped up and he caught his breath at her serene beauty. "I brought your bag up. I should go to work. You stay this time. Understand?"

She nodded, blinking slowly. As she stretched and yawned, the sheet slid to her waist. Her breasts mounded as she raised her arms over head. She brought her arms down around his neck and pulled him to her lips. With her hands stroking the back of his neck, she gazed into his face trustingly.

"Oh, baby, you're wicked," he moaned. He buried his face in the hollow of her neck, inhaling her scent, muted by and mingled with his own. With superhuman effort, he lifted his head.

"I've got to go. Please let me go," he implored, clenching his jaw.

Sabrina luxuriated in her power for a few seconds, and then let her arms drop. She wiggled deeper into his pillows, her lips curving into a satisfied, mysterious smile. She listened as Jay moved through the apartment, pulling on his work boots, gathering his wallet and keys, and then closing the door softly. She heard his muffled footsteps as he raced down the stairs.

When she opened her eyes again, the clock read 10:20.

ROBIN VAN AUKEN

She heard machines buzzing in the distance and the occasional clang as a tool dropped. A radio played loud rock 'n' roll. Jay was at work in the boatyard below.

She saw her overnight bag and purse at the foot of the bed and decided she needed a shower. She took her time, first exploring the small cabinets and closets in the bathroom. Even this room looks like a sailboat, she thought, peeking behind the teak doors and noting the sparse contents. She opened her bag and withdrew her toiletries.

Thank goodness I brought my toothbrush, she thought, squeezing the tube of paste. Her bathroom ritual took considerable more time than Jay's, and by 11:30 she was showered, her hair dried and styled. She had to make do with wrinkled clothes. She couldn't find an iron anywhere. How can some people not own one? All her life she had fastidiously ironed her clothes before wearing them. She hung her jeans and shirt over the shower bar and ran the hot water, hoping to steam some of the wrinkles free.

Once dressed, she realized she was famished. She poked in the cabinets in the kitchenette. The coffee was cold, and there was no creamer. The refrigerator was nearly empty, also.

"How does this man survive?" she spoke aloud.

Sabrina decided to head for the coffee shop where she'd lunched her first day in town. She couldn't find her car keys, though. She frowned, trying to recall where she had left them.

She stuffed her clothes and toiletries in her bag and walked barefoot down the stairs. She saw he moved her car, so she opened the driver's door. Tossing her bags on the seat, she looked in the ignition, under the floor mat, even the visor.

"Looking for these?"

She jumped, bumping her head on the liner. "Ouch," she said, rubbing her forehead and turning slowly. Jay leaned against the fender, her keys in his outstretched hand. She slid out of the car and when she reached for her keys, he tucked them in the front pocket of his jeans.

"Thought I told you to stay put," he said.

Sabrina rolled her eyes. "Maybe if you had some food, a girl would stick around." She sidled up to him, wrapping her arms around his waist, lifting her head to nuzzle his chin. "I'll be back," she murmured. "I'm starved." She wiggled her fingers into his pocket and withdrew her keys.

"Besides," she said as she slid in the car, "I need you. You've got my boat."

Jay leaned in before she could close the door. "Is that why you need me?"

Sabrina grinned. "You want me to stroke your ego?"

"Among other things," he said.

She whispered in his ear and kissed him goodbye, but since Jay didn't speak Portuguese, he couldn't know that she described, in explicit detail, what she needed.

"I hope that was a compliment," he said.

"Oh, it was, me amo."

He grimaced as she fought the wheel of the large car and drove inexpertly down the alley and into the on-coming, honking traffic.

"City girls."

Back in the shop, Brett was putting a tarp over a wooden hull he had been sanding.

"Hey, you took Spanish in high school, didn't you?"

"That was a long time ago, bud."

"What does 'me amo' mean?"

"Run like hell," Brett replied.

CHAPTER THIRTEEN

Faye West stomped through her kitchen, still dressed in a bathrobe and slippers. It was after two o'clock and she had just watched a "shock" talk show episode titled "Are You My Baby's Daddy?" It featured a young, overweight woman, her infant, and three men, similarly dressed in oversized T-shirts, baggy pants with crotches that hung down to their knees, and baseball caps turned sideways. The men had submitted to DNA testing and, surprise, surprise, none of them were the "baby's daddy."

"Slut," Faye grumbled, lighting a cigarette and then opening the refrigerator. She looked inside for the seventh time that afternoon, not hungry because of nicotine and caffeine, but knowing she had to eat. Faye weighed about ninety pounds but she claimed she didn't have an eating disorder. She just wasn't interested in food. She wasn't interested in much of anything.

Except Jay. She picked up the portable telephone and called the boatyard.

On the other end, Brett noted the caller ID and whistled to Jay. "It's your grandmother."

"Don't answer," Jay responded, then went back to

spraying primer on the bottom of a boat. "I've got to finish this coat or I'll have to start all over."

Over the compressor, Jay heard Faye leave a long and rambling message, although he couldn't make out the words. He realized, guiltily, that he generally had dinner with Faye once a week and missed it last night. One thought diverged to another and he recalled how he spent last night.

Faye slammed the telephone back onto its base and walked to the kitchen window. She still lived in the same house Derek West built for them on the Warren River, although it was beginning to look rundown compared to her neighbors' homes. She didn't want to think about it, didn't want to think about the fact that the yard needed mowing or that the gutters were full of leaves. When Jay lived with her, he kept the house maintained. Now, with the boatyard and his own place, he barely had time for his grandmother anymore, she thought.

She called back and once again, the men ignored her telephone call. "I need you to come and take care of the lawn," she told the answering machine, "and look at the garage door, too. Something's not right. Stupid remote doesn't work anymore."

Faye suffered from depression and never sought help. Instead, after the betrayal and death of her husband, and the subsequent addiction and death of her daughter, Faye retreated into a familiar world of bitterness.

Jealousy consumed her as a young wife and she detested the bright and beautiful Rose Windham. Fair haired, blue eyed, educated and wealthy, Rose was everything Faye wasn't. She even had a roly-poly son who gurgled and bounced on his daddy's shoulders, while Faye delivered a premature, sickly and demanding daughter. Faye thought Derek was disappointed; he wanted his first born to be a son. Derek looked up to Don Windham and wanted everything his older friend had.

That included Rose Windham, and it cost him his life.

In reality, Margaret was a beautiful little girl and Derek had been thrilled with his small family, but the insecure Faye imagined intrigue and unhappiness where none existed. And when it did exist, after more than ten years of accusations, Faye's bitter anguish became vindication.

She detested Rose Windham still, blaming her for Derek's death and for Margaret's. If the young girl's father had been around, she would not have turned to drugs and alcohol, Faye reasoned. The girl wouldn't have gotten pregnant at the age of seventeen, would have finished high school and made something of herself.

Faye gazed despondently out her kitchen window and waited for the telephone to ring. Waited for the only person in the world she loved, and the only person who loved her, to call. She stood in the kitchen unmoving for more than an hour until the telephone rang. She smiled skeletally.

Later that afternoon, Jay took a break and went upstairs to his apartment. Sabrina hadn't come back, and he wanted to see if she'd left anything behind, a sign she may return.

The apartment was silent and empty, shadowy. Sabrina straightened the bed before she left and her scent lingered in the bathroom. Jay stood in the bedroom for several minutes, his eyes closed as he savored the memory of Sabrina's goodbye kiss.

Unbidden, his thoughts turned to Faye and he flinched. He returned her call and agreed to have dinner with her the following evening. He also promised to stop by on Saturday, mow the lawn, and check her air conditioner. Normally, he didn't mind Faye's demands, but now that Sabrina had materialized, he resented having to choose. He also didn't look forward to keeping the two women apart.

His apartment phone rang and he checked the caller ID before picking up the receiver.

"Yeah, Brett?"

"Hey, Sabrina is on line one. She's at the grocery store. You want I should tell her to take a hike?"

"Nah, I'll talk to her. Put her through."

He waited as Brett cycled the telephone system and soon he heard her breathy voice. "Hello, Jay?"

"Hey. Taking the day off?" he teased.

Sabrina shifted her cell phone to her shoulder and reached into her purse for the Cadillac keys. "Busted. Let me make it up to you. I was wondering if you'd like to have dinner this evening. Maybe someplace a bit more intimate than Maude's?"

"Where were you thinking?"

"Well, what do you suggest?" She unlocked the trunk of the car and placed shopping bags inside.

Jay played the game. "Why don't you come here and we'll have dinner at my place?"

Sabrina slid behind the wheel and started the Cadillac's engine. "That could be arranged if you like steak with red wine, salad, bisque soup and ice cream for dessert."

Jay disconnected and went downstairs to the boat shop.

"Well, old buddy, you've worked hard enough today," he said, slapping Brett on the back. "Take off. I'll see you tomorrow."

Brett shook his head. "I can't go home now. Shawna will think I've been fired."

"Go fishing, then."

Jay walked through the shop, turning off lights and cutting switches to the table saw and other heavy equipment.

"All right," Brett conceded. "I'm going. You know, I could close up the shop if you want to take off."

Jay shook his head and pointedly opened the front door. "No thanks."

He went to the street entrance and slid the large, chain-link gate closed, securing it with a padlock. He set the burglar alarm, and went to his loft apartment, taking the stairs two at a time. Inside, he quickly stripped and jumped into the shower. He was lathering his hair when he heard the apartment door bang open, followed by a few more thumps. He was rinsing the shampoo when the shower door slid open and a frisky hand slid up his belly.

"Hey!" he yelped.

Sabrina's face appeared in the opening, mischievously smiling, a dimple in her soft, round cheek. "You could have helped me with the groceries, you know," she chided as she pulled off her shirt. Her shoes and pants followed and within seconds, she was standing in the shower between Jay and the spray, still clad in her underwear. She picked up the bar of soap and rubbed it on his chest.

Jay kissed her gently, his hands resting on her hips. "Thought I'd be finished by the time you got back."

"And deny me all this fun?"

"What about the ice cream?"

"I put it in the freezer. The rest can wait," she said, her bold hands sliding lower. "Mmmmm. You missed me."

"It's that obvious, huh?" Jay chucked and slid her bra straps down her shoulders, planting kisses along the tops of her round, wet breasts. He swiveled her so she was out of the spray then sank to his knees, his arms wrapped around her hips. His hot mouth seared her skin as he tongued her belly and thighs. He pulled her panties down to her ankles and, as she stepped out of them, he pressed his mouth against her. With her hands trembling in his wet hair, Sabrina swooned and leaned against the tile wall. He held her tight, cupping her bottom as he lick and bit and plunged his tongue into her velvet softness. He relished her taste, reveled in the feel of her as she hardened against his mouth.

Sabrina slung one leg over his shoulder and pulled him closer with fisted hands. His fingers were free to roam her wet body and caress her breasts. When he tweaked her nipples, Sabrina whimpered and ground against his mouth. Soon she was panting and begging for release.

"Let go, sweetheart," he whispered.

Sabrina moaned and erupted, pushing him away as she sank slowly from heaven. The only thing holding her up was her leg, wrapped around Jay's neck. She thought she would be mortified as she looked down into his grinning face, but instead she giggled.

"You're crazy, you know that?" She caressed his face, her fingers sliding through his short beard and mustache. "And, don't ever get rid of this," she commanded.

It was dark by the time they emerged from Jay's bedroom, groggy and relaxed from their tantric lovemaking. He considered falling asleep but when Sabrina whispered in his ear that she was hungry, he followed her into the kitchen.

Dressed in one of his shirts, the sleeves rolled up and the buttons off center, she opened the refrigerator and pulled out the grocery bags.

Jay sat on a barstool and spooned ice cream into his mouth while Sabrina broiled steaks and concocted a salad. The soup was ready-made, so she popped it in the microwave.

"You're pretty quick, aren't you?" he noted.

"When you live alone, you become efficient. This is one of my favorite meals, so I've streamlined the process. See? While I broil the steaks for six minutes on each side, I pour salad from a bag, sprinkle on the blue cheese crumbles and chopped walnuts, then slice the pear and, voila, all it needs is salad dressing. Dang, I forgot to buy dressing." She rummaged through his refrigerator. "Do you have any?"

Jay nodded, his mouth full of chocolate ice cream. Sabrina, of course, couldn't hear anything except a mumbled reply so she scavenged the refrigerator door until she found a nearly empty bottle.

"Italian. My favorite," she said and dumped the contents into the salad bowl.

Seven minutes later, she speared the sizzling steaks onto the plates and filled glasses with red wine. With a flourish, Sabrina plunked two bowls of steaming bisque on the counter beside the salad and tore chunks off a fresh loaf of bread.

Jay reached for a knife and fork then paused while Sabrina bowed her head and moved her lips.

"Are you okay? What are you doing?"

She looked up and laughed. "Saying grace, silly. Don't you pray?"

Jay scratched his head in jest, slightly unnerved. "No, not really."

"Well, I'm a good Catholic girl, so I pray all the time. Hopefully, it will make up for the premarital sex and birth control," she quipped.

Speechless, Jay's mouth dropped open.

Sabrina laughed again and shoved his shoulder. "Eat your dinner, Jay. I'll pray for you, too."

Later that night, back in the king-sized bed, Sabrina spooned against Jay's back and stroked his hair. "Jay?" she whispered. "Are you awake?"

He didn't reply, and the rhythmic rise and fall of his shoulders assured her that he slept deeply. Confident he couldn't hear, but needing to say her feelings aloud, Sabrina murmured in the dark. Nervous and shy, she spoke in her mother's language, Portuguese, so even if Jay had been awake, he wouldn't have understood. In a soothing, soft voice, she told his sleeping back what she could not say to his face.

She held her breath when he stirred and rolled over. He tossed an arm across her hips and tucked his head. His breath fanned her chilled skin and she shivered. It was easy to imagine being in his arms forever, wanting to belong to him, wanting a family. She closed her eyes and pictured a baby with chestnut curls and blue eyes and her heart ached.

It also frightened her, this intense yearning for someone she barely knew. Yet, she acknowledged, she did know him. What she felt for him, and what he certainly must feel for her, seemed light years beyond the crush she had on Robert Hall, or her relationship with Jeremy Rice, her former fiancé.

But what if he doesn't want me? What if he doesn't feel the way I do? What if he's not in love with me?

Sabrina stifled the urge to wake Jay, to prod him to make love to her again because she realized the need was born of fear and desperation. Intellectually, she knew that sex couldn't be the only bond between them. She willed herself to relax, to breathe and to stop worrying. Soon she slept, not waking until Jay's alarm clock buzzed.

CHAPTER FOURTEEN

The following morning, Jay and Sabrina sat at the kitchen bar and drank coffee. Jay scrambled eggs and toasted bagels for breakfast, but she was too nervous to eat.

"I need to go to Eaton this weekend," Sabrina said, twisting her long, dark hair into a knot at the back of her head. "I should be there for Grandmother. Don't worry; I'll come back to work on the boat."

Jay sipped his coffee. "I thought you said she was in the hospital."

"She is," Sabrina replied, picking up her cup. "But I still need to be there. I'm the only family she has."

"What about your parents?"

"They're still in Tibet. They won't return for another two weeks. Besides, they don't count." She slammed her cup on the counter.

"What do you mean, 'they don't count?' "

"They're not close to Grandmother Rose. They never have been. My father went to boarding schools and then went to college out of state."

"Like you did," he observed, sipping coffee.

"Yes, but it was different with me. I spent my summers

114

with Grandmother Rose. Honestly, if you think about it, I've probably spent more time with her than with Mom and Dad."

"You're not close to your parents?"

"It's their choice, not mine," she said defensively. "Sometimes I think they would have preferred a dog. A pet they could keep in a kennel."

Jay put his cup on the mahogany counter and wrapped his arms around Sabrina. "Hey, it's all right, honey," he said, kissing her tenderly. "Don't cry."

"I'm not," she said, sniffling. "It just makes me mad, that's all. If I ever have children, I'm never leaving them behind." She swayed into his embrace, her eyes closed.

He rocked her gently, waiting for her tears to subside. When she sniffed, and started to pull away, Jay took her hands in his. "Would you like me to go with you?"

Sabrina recoiled. "You? Go to Pennsylvania with me? You want to meet Grandmother?"

"Well, not if you don't want me to," he said, reading her body language.

"No, it's not that. I just thought ... well, that you...," her voice became a whisper, "...wouldn't want to meet my family."

She lifted nervous eyes to his.

"I'll do whatever you want me to do, Sabrina. Whatever will make you happy," he said.

"Say that again," she commanded.

"Whatever you want," he replied, cupping her head and sliding his hand through her hair, loosening her ponytail. He caught her trembling bottom lip between his own. "If it makes you happy," he murmured against her open mouth, his tongue teasing hers.

Sabrina's heart thumped heavily, tears beaded her lashes and slid down her cheeks. Jay tasted the salt and groaned. "Why are you still crying?"

"Because I'm happy."

* * *

"You sure you can trust me with the shop for three days? Earlier this week, you couldn't even rely on me to close it," Brett teased Jay the following morning.

"Don't be a wise ass. I trust you. I just didn't want you around. Besides, we're not open on Saturday and Sunday, so it's only two days."

"What about Faye? Weren't you going to have dinner there tonight?" Brett reminded.

Jay flinched. "Ah crap. I'm going to have to cancel. Listen, the lawn needs mowing. Think you can do that on Saturday?"

"No, but I can do it on Sunday. The in-laws are coming by and that's a good time to cut loose."

"Thanks. I appreciate it. I guess I'd better call her."

Jay retreated into his small, private office with the portable telephone and called Faye. She answered on the first ring.

"Grandma, it's me, Jay."

"I know. I got the caller ID."

"Look, I've got to go out of town for a couple of days. I can't come to dinner tonight. Also, Brett is going to come by on Sunday to mow your lawn, so don't worry about that."

"Where you going?" Faye demanded.

"Client of mine needs to consult about a project," Jay said, not quite lying. Sabrina is a client, he reasoned.

"Well, when you going to be back?"

"Monday, probably late," he added, realizing she could still finagle dinner with him.

"Harrumph." Faye hated to be frustrated and had a sneaking suspicion that Jay was avoiding her. "Call me when you get back now, you hear?"

"Yes, Grandma," he said, his mild tone calming Faye's mounting anxiety. "Get some rest. I'll see you in a few days."

He hung up the telephone and shuddered. He detested lying to Faye, but the woman was clinging and often unreasonable. Still, he was all the family she had and Jay felt responsible not only for her well-being, but for her happiness. He knew that the only thing that made her happy was his presence at her table, or working on some project in her small, decrepit house.

She liked to imagine that he was still a teen and living at home. She blithely ignored the fact that he ran away from her and home as a teen, living on his own for more than fifteen years.

Jay slung his duffle bag across his shoulder and headed for the shop door. "Thanks, Brett. I appreciate this," he said.

"No problem, brother."

"All right, then. You've got my cell phone number, so call me if you need me. Mr. Corder will be by later this afternoon with his trailer to pick up the 30-footer. The invoice is on the board in the office."

"Got it, Cap'n. Have a good time."

"What else?" Jay murmured, looking around the shop. The two men, friends for years, worked with precision and both kept the small boatyard in good working order. They generally worked ahead on each project, so there weren't many loose ends.

Brett threw a shop rag at Jay. "Would you get out of here? It's under control."

Jay saluted the assistant manager and left the shop, striding through the boatyard and to the street. A nervous Sabrina leaned against the blue Cadillac, twisting her car keys. Jay bent and kissed her, wrapping a large, warm hand around her anxious fingers.

"Want me to drive?"

"Oh, yes, would you? I'm not very experienced, and I've decided I hate Connecticut's traffic more than New York's," she said, handing him the keys. He opened the passenger door and she slid in with a sigh of relief.

CHAPTER FIFTEEN

Eight hours later, Jay whistled as he drove down a shady Pennsylvania street. He admired the Victorian mansions. "Pretty town," he observed. "Nice houses."

"Eaton was a wealthy town in the 1800s," Sabrina explained. "Many of the coal barons lived in these mansions, competing to see who could build the fanciest house. Most of these homes were designed by the same architect."

Jay grinned. "You sound like a tour guide."

"I like history. On my twelfth birthday, Grandmother sent me the official county history. It was written in 1894, so it's not exactly current."

She guided him to the alley and he parked in the garage. They walked to the front of the home so Jay could see Rose Windham's house from the street. Sabrina glowed as he admired the professionally painted gingerbread trim and the white wicker furniture on the expansive front porch. The gardener updated the landscape for the summer, placing lush ferns along the balustrade. The porch included a hammock on a metal stand and a swing. Floral pillows graced the furniture.

Jay inwardly flinched. He couldn't prevent himself from comparing the wealth, beauty and ease that Rose Windham enjoyed while his own grandmother, Faye West, moped in a small, one-story tract house with faded asbestos siding, a broken garage door and an air conditioner that worked sporadically. He silently vowed to visit Faye on his return and tend to the chores he'd neglected.

Sabrina unlocked the front door and punched a code into the alarm system. The panel flashed green and she closed the door behind them. The house was hushed and gloomy. Sabrina walked through the first-floor rooms and lifted shades, opened curtains and let the sunshine pour into the stylish interior. Jay said nothing, his mouth grim as he followed Sabrina. He was careful not to touch any of the precious vases or statues, and wondered how someone could live in a house full of elegant antique furniture.

"She likes roses, doesn't she?"

"It's a theme," Sabrina explained. "All of the Victorian mansions along this street are part of the historic preservation plan for the town and are open twice a year for the historic homes tour. They do it once in December, with houses decorated for the holidays, and again in the summer, when the gardens are in bloom. This house has an English country garden and a rose-themed interior. The house next door is a Tudor style with heavy, dark British furniture. It belongs to Dr. Finkelstein, who teaches English at the college, so his theme is Shakespeare. He has a large corner lot where the community theater stages Shakespeare plays during the summer."

Sabrina continued, "Across the street is Alfredo Dante's house and it has an Italian design. See, each house is different and decorated along a theme that is unique to the owner."

Jay nodded. "Sounds nice," he said. "But why are you nervous?"

Sabrina didn't want to admit that she hadn't told Rose

about Jay coming to Pennsylvania. She worried about their impending introduction.

"I'm not," she said with a false bravado. "Really, I'm fine. Let's go upstairs. I'll show you my room."

"That's what I've been waiting for," he joked and picked up their bags. He kept his eyes on her back as she mounted the steps. When she opened the door to her bedroom, he squinted.

"It's yellow," was all he could say, overwhelmed by the femininity. He dropped the bags and turned his back to the bed. "Come here," he murmured, pulling Sabrina into his arms and collapsing on the bed. He rubbed his hands on her rounded bottom, clutching her to him. He groaned in pleasure and his mouth sought her neck.

Sabrina planted her hands on his shoulders and sinuously squirmed against him. "You're the first boy I've ever snuck into my bedroom," she whispered.

"Ever?" he mumbled against her shirt, pulling buttons loose with his teeth. He refused to let go of her bottom, gently maneuvering her against him. His tongue snaked beneath her bra and laved a hardened nipple. Sabrina hissed in appreciation.

"You shouldn't tease me," she said, rising to sit astride him. He watched with interest as she unbuttoned her shirt and removed it. She reached behind and unsnapped her bra, let it slide down her arms, then tossed it into a corner. Jay sighed, admiring her honey-hued breasts crowned with cinnamon. Sabrina leaned over him, her hands beside his ears, and let one breast swing close to his lips. He lifted his head, opened his mouth and encircled her nipple. His hands slid up her belly and reached for the snap at the waistband of her jeans.

She flipped her dark, soft hair to one side, an ebony waterfall that flowed onto Jay's shoulder. Supporting herself with one hand, she used the other to reach between them and unbutton Jay's jeans. Soon, she freed him from his boxers and encircled him with eager fingers. She stroked, sliding her hand up and down until he felt like steel.

Meanwhile, Jay's fingers were on their own quest, pushing her jeans down her hips and pushing aside the wisp of fabric between her thighs. She was wet and warm against his palm. Sabrina's hips began a rhythmic surrender. With their jeans pushed to their ankles, they arched towards each other until velvet enclosed steel. Raising his hips, he entered effortlessly and their bodies sealed.

Sabrina's knees clasped his hips, her hands splayed on his chest. Jay supported her with one hand on the small of her back while the other stroked her belly and breasts. His fingers traced back to the dark triangle between their sweating bodies and he caressed her. Frantic, Sabrina increased her pace, sliding up and down and squeezing until Jay gasped and went rigid. She nearly screamed her pleasure, biting her lip at the last moment and groaning instead.

Slowly she sank, her flushed cheek resting against Jay's chest, still covered with his black T-shirt. The absurdity of their loving struggle, the fact that they refused to take the time to undress, made her giggle.

"I amuse you?" Jay murmured against her hair, stroking her naked back.

"Yes, you do," Sabrina said. "We're crazy, don't you think?"

"Probably. It would explain how I ended up in a yellow frilly bedroom with my pants around my ankles with a woman I've only known a week."

Sabrina giggled again and struggled to sit up. Instead, she rolled over and straightened her clothes. While she reached for her discarded bra and shirt, Jay recovered his jeans and snapped them easily. "Wait," he said, pulling her towards him. "Don't get dressed yet."

Sabrina paused, her shirt and bra in one hand, her other secure in Jay's palm. He settled her between his knees and rubbed his face on her belly. She dropped her clothing and wrapped her arms around him tenderly.

"Is something wrong?" she asked, resting her cheek on the top of his head.

"No, honey, everything's just right," he said, nuzzling her heavy breasts. "This is nice and you smell great. You're beautiful and I can't keep my hands off you."

"That's good. I want your hands on me," she whispered, closing her eyes as he sucked tenderly on one breast, then the other, rolling her firm nipples between his lips. "And your mouth," she added.

"You like it when I touch you, don't you?" he gently teased.

"I love it." Her passionate response startled him at first, then he felt a rush of possession.

Sabrina cupped his face and lifted it to meet her lips. She kissed him, pouring her heart into the gesture. "But you'd better let me get dressed, or else...."

"I think 'or else' is a better idea. I could use a nap about now; couldn't you?" he bent over and untied her shoes and tugged them off, and then unsnapped her jeans again and slid them down her hips. "I think a nap is exactly what you need," he affirmed.

When he had her naked, he pulled her lush body against his and stretched out on her bed. "What about your clothes?" Sabrina asked.

"I'm fine," he said, yawning. He closed his eyes and explored her bare skin. Sabrina felt erotic and wicked, lying atop the bed nude, her skin tingling at the touch of his lightly callused hands and clothing. His T-shirt was soft to the touch, his jeans worn smooth.

"Quit wiggling and go to sleep," he said, a teasing smile tugging at his mouth.

"I can't," she confessed. "You're doing this on purpose."

"Doing what?" he murmured, his eyes closed.

"You know very well what," she said and tucked his

hand between her thighs. She pushed against his palm and sighed rapturously when his fingers began their feathering tempo.

She wiggled up his body, his face buried between her breasts. "Kiss me," she demanded, her hand cupping the back of his neck.

Jay complied, kissing and suckling one breast then the other, gently tugging and biting her engorged nipples while his fingers stroked Sabrina into submission. The slow and sensuous caress drove her to the brink and over, and she hugged him tightly.

"Okay," she conceded, fluttering to earth. "I'll take that nap now."

Sabrina poked around in the kitchen while Jay took a shower. He came downstairs, his uncombed hair wet and shining. He tucked a clean shirt into his jeans, then raked his unruly hair.

"That's it? You're good to go?" Sabrina marveled. "Why is it that men can take a five-minute shower, wear old, wrinkled clothes and still look like a hunk? Women spend at least an hour getting ready and we still don't like the way we look."

Jay shrugged.

She slammed the cabinet door. "Well, there's nothing to eat except six cans of chicken noodle soup. That does it. I'm going to take a bath while you call for pizza."

She headed up the stairs, and called over her shoulder. "Would you check the wine cellar and pick out a bottle of red? Order extra cheese and pepperoni, too." As an afterthought, she added, "Please."

"I thought you wanted to get to the hospital," he stalled.

"I do, but visiting hours are from six to eight. We've got at least an hour," she replied from the landing. "The telephone number is on the speed dial. Just punch 'memory six.' "

The disembodied voice on the end of the line put Jay on hold for several minutes, then came back, repeated the order and told him it would be at least 20 minutes before the food arrived.

After he hung up the telephone, Jay searched for the basement door, finding it at the end of the hall. The staircase was steep and the walls musty and draped with cobwebs. He found a furnace, some rusty garden tools and a box of mildewed newspapers. No wine cellar. He hiked up the stairs to Sabrina's second-floor private bath, opened the door and perched on the side of the old claw foot tub.

"Okay, I give. Where's the wine cellar," he asked.

"It's in the kitchen pantry. Grandmother had a temperature-controlled unit installed in the kitchen years ago. Where did you think it was?" Sabrina relaxed in the deep water filled with fragrant bubbles. She dimpled. "Oh, you went into the basement, didn't you? Ewww; there are spiders down there."

She reached up and stroked his head. "You have cobwebs in your hair," she said, shaking her fingers, trying to rid them of the sticky threads.

Jay contemplated pulling off his clothes and climbing into the oversized tub for his second bath of the day, but the doorbell rang. Sabrina brightened and stood, water cascading down her body. "Pizza!"

She tugged a soft towel from a nearby bar and wrapped it around her torso, tucking the corner over her left breast. She shoved at Jay, immobile on the side of the tub. "Quit staring and go get the pizza," she bossed. "I'll be right down."

Jay sighed then stomped down the stairs. He yanked open the door as the impatient delivery boy's finger hovered at the bell. Pulling out his wallet, he said, "How much?"

"Sixteen-fifty," the teen said as he leaned to the right, looking around Jay and at the beautiful young woman skipping down the steps in panties and a T-shirt. Jay glanced over his shoulder, then shoved a twenty into the kid's hand, grabbed the pizza box and slammed the door in his face.

Grinning, Sabrina tugged the box from his grip and headed down the hallway to the kitchen. She placed it on the table, then opened a cabinet and withdrew plates. Then she pulled a couple of wine glasses from a hanging rack. She nodded her head towards an oak door. "Here's the wine cellar," she said. "What do you think? A shiraz? A zinfandel? Anything but merlot, please."

Jay flipped open the pizza box and watched as steam rose. "Couldn't tell you, sweetheart. I'm not a wine connoisseur."

She opened the wide, nickel-plated refrigerator. "How about a beer? We have lager or ale."

Folding a slice of pizza and lifting it to his mouth, he paused long enough to say, "Lager," then bit off half.

"Save some for me, piggy," Sabrina said, sliding into a kitchen chair. She twisted the caps off two lagers and handed him one. Then she watched apprehensively as he lifted the bottle and chugged. "What's with you tonight?"

Jay set the bottle on the table and picked up his pizza again. "Nothing," he said. "I'm fine. Just not used to all this toff."

Once again, Sabrina felt the stab of the haves versus the have-nots. "It doesn't really mean anything," she assured him.

"As I said before, money's never a problem for those who have it," Jay said nonchalantly.

"And I'm a 'poor little rich girl,' right?"

"Would I have ever met you if it weren't for your money?" he asked, his voice low and dangerous.

Sabrina's head whipped. "Absolutely not! And you mean, if it weren't for Rose's money, because I don't have much of my own. She wouldn't have met Don Windham, either, without the money. They never would have married and maybe he wouldn't have built a boatyard with your grandfather. My father and I would never have been born. Perhaps you never would have been born. Who knows what affect money has and who knows where it begins or ends?"

She climbed into his lap, forcing him to abandon his beer and pizza. Snuggling against his chest, her arms draped around his neck, she said, "But we can choose how we let it affect us. In the past few weeks, I've learned some ugly truths about people abusing each other in the name of love and money. Don Windham rejected Rose's fortune, forcing her to break with her father. His obsession and selfish determination drove her into another man's arms."

Jay stiffened at her words. "That other man was my grandfather. Maybe her selfishness and greed drove her husband away. Don't for a minute think it was some tragic love story."

Sabrina sighed. "No, you're right," she said, softly kissing his cheek. "She knows she was wrong and she lives with the guilt. Their blood is on her hands. I believe she suffers."

Jay looked around at the opulence and scoffed. "This isn't suffering." He pulled her arms from his neck, pushed her from his lap and stood. "Being betrayed and then widowed is suffering. Living as a crack whore is suffering. Watching your own mother kill herself with drugs and alcohol is suffering."

"You're right; you win. Your family suffered while mine enjoyed their luxurious lives. A guilt-ridden widow shunning family and friends, a lonely, confused little boy shuttled off to military school, and a burdensome daughter that nobody wanted. But all of that's okay because at least we could cry into silken pillows, right?"

She shoved from the table and wrapped her arms around her stomach. "Why are we arguing? Because I suggested wine for dinner? Do you see how crazy this is? One small thing leads to another and gets blown out of proportion."

She approached his back, wrapping her arms around his waist, resting her cheek on his shoulder. "We don't have to let their craziness affect us. I've just found you. Let's enjoy this. Enjoy being together. Don't push me away."

He didn't want to, but he could feel Faye's venom in his veins, the poison closing down his heart. How could he be here, amid the elegance and refinement of Rose Windham's home when Faye's old house was practically falling to pieces, the air conditioner a piece of junk, the lawn overgrown and full of weeds. And Faye, an anorexic, cigarette-puffing harridan, all because of a bored prep woman's whim. Seduce another woman's husband to make her own sit up and take notice.

As chaotic thoughts rushed through his mind, he felt Sabrina caressing his chest, tugging at his heart, as if her fingers could push through skin, through muscle and heal him. He turned in her embrace and clutched her, rocked her against him.

"I'm sorry," he whispered against her glossy head. "All my life, all I've ever heard is bitterness and hate for the Windhams. Not you. Rose Windham. Sometimes I think it's the only thing keeping Faye alive. Her bitterness."

Sabrina stroked his cheek and shed tears for the little orphaned boy who grew up with a twisted, angry grandmother. "You have to let the bitterness go," she whispered. "We have something special and I know it's too soon, but I can't help feel this way. I love you and I wouldn't want anything, or anyone, to hurt you."

Her simple, heartfelt admission humbled him. He cupped her face and kissed her, a groan of defeat tearing his throat.

"I'm going to get dressed and go visit Rose," she whispered against his lips. "Do you want to go with me?"

He nodded, his forehead resting on her silken shoulder.

* * *

Jay stood in the doorway of the hospital room, watching as Sabrina knelt at the bedside. One gentle hand clasped Rose's frail white fingers while the other smoothed the blanket, stroking the old woman as if she were a beloved pet. Sabrina glanced over her shoulder at Jay. She murmured and nodded. He advanced.

Rose's blue eyes lifted from her granddaughter to the giant towering over her bed. Tears filled then flowed down her sunken, wrinkled cheek. She lifted a wavering hand.

"You're so like him," she whispered. "You're so handsome."

Jay's eyes darted from Rose to Sabrina. He cocked an eyebrow at the word "handsome."

Rose continued, "So like her. Such a lovely girl, your mother." Her head lolled to the side sadly. "I'm sorry. Please forgive me. I took everything from you."

He didn't know how to answer so he stood silent, stoic. Sabrina reached for his hand and squeezed it.

"Grandmother, we're going back to Rhode Island on Monday. Jay runs a boatyard there. I won't be gone long," she promised.

Rose blinked, nodding her head once. "Yes, yes, go. Don't fret. I've got all these doctors and nurses hovering around. There's nothing to worry about."

Jay watched the exchange between grandparent and grandchild and thought, this is how it's supposed to be. No screaming and slapping. No drugs and alcohol.

Sabrina thought she was unloved as a child but he could see it pouring from the old woman. A worshipful love for the only person in the tangled web not damaged by Rose's selfish, destructive past. It was hard to recall his hatred, his rage while looking at the fragile old woman, silently weeping as she caressed them both with her strange pale eyes. Silently apologizing for the ruin she caused. He felt a lightness and couldn't help himself as he placed a reassuring hand on her arm. She reached over, trailing an I.V. tube, and patted his hand, smiling tremulously.

The next morning, Sabrina pulled out the boxes filled with old letters and journals and they lounged on the side porch for hours, reading about their grandparents' lives.

"Look at this photo of Don and Derek," Sabrina said, handing Jay a small black-and-white photo with scalloped edges. "You really do look like him."

Jay studied the photo. "I've never seen one before," he murmured.

Sabrina looked up from the box, curious. "You've never seen a photo of your grandfather?"

He shook his head. "No, Faye burned them all. There's nothing left."

Placing a hand on his knee, she said, "Well, I'll share my booty with you. Rose gave me permission to keep anything I want. And believe me, this is the last thing my father would want. He and Mom have each other and their Tibetan yaks, or whatever they ride over there."

Jay tucked the photo into his wallet. "Thanks."

He'd been quiet since they started the ransack, reading about the Windhams and the Wests through the perspective of the young, beautiful and wealthy Rose. He tapped a box. "Is this the last of it?"

Sabrina looked inside and saw a cache of letters tied in lavender ribbon. "Yes, this is the end. These letters are from the final year. There's a newspaper clipping of the fire …." she said, halting as Jay stood and stretched.

"I'll look at it later," he said. "I'm getting restless. Let's take a walk."

"Sure," she said, rising gracefully. "Where would you like to go?"

"Anywhere. Just not here," he growled, looking around at flouncy pillows and vases. "Too stuffy. Too many flowers."

She slipped into a pair of sneakers and fisted the car keys. "I know just the place," she said. "But we need to drive there."

Fifteen minutes later, she pulled onto a winding country road. "How far up this mountain are you going to go?" Jay asked.

"Not much further. Hold your horses."

They rounded a switchback in the road and she pulled onto a beaten patch. "You're going to like this," she promised, turning off the car but leaving the keys in the ignition.

"Don't you want to take those with you?" he asked.

"Nah, this is the country. People don't bother locking up here. Come on, follow me."

They walked a game trail between a low cliff and a stand of hemlocks until it opened to a glorious waterfall spilling into a deep, quiet pool. The roar of falling water pounded his eardrums. Then a bird sang, and another and soon the tree frogs began chirping to each other. It didn't take long before nature welcomed them as one of her own.

He reverently took her hand. "What is this place?"

Sabrina pulled him to the ground, sitting on a flat, sunny rock. "This is Weeping Woman Mountain," she said. "And that is Weeping Woman Falls. There's an old Indian legend of a warrior who died in battle and his wife wept for weeks at the top of this mountain. When she finally threw herself off, the gods took pity and lifted her to heaven to be with him. As a memorial to her love, they turned her tears into this waterfall."

She looked at him and rolled her eyes. "Yeah, I know. It's hokey. There's always an Indian legend of star-crossed lovers leaping to death. This one is my favorite."

Jay stretched out on the rock, resting his hands on his stomach. He studied the clouds, watching as the billowy white puffs floated through the treetops. The gentle rush of water soothed him and he knew this is what he missed: Water.

He detested being inland. It had been two days and already the saltwater was drying in his veins. He rolled to his side, propped his head on a hand and watched Sabrina explore.

She dipped her toes in the pool, searched for tadpoles and occasionally looked over at Jay. She picked wildflowers and brought them to the rock, sitting cross-legged in the sunshine. "We used to make flower necklaces at school," she said, concentrating on weaving stalks. She made a small loop and held it up for inspection. "More like a crown instead of a necklace," she said, laying it on Jay's head. Then she reclined next to him, laying on her stomach. With her chin on her knuckles, she studied him. He hadn't said anything in the past half hour; just watched her frolic by the pool.

He traced a finger down her elegant nose, over her lush lips and lifted her chin, leaning in for a kiss. Closing his eyes and rubbing his unshaven cheek against hers, he said, "Will you marry me?"

Sabrina blinked. "Is this the definition of whirlwind romance?"

"Well, you said you love me."

"Yes," she admitted, sitting up and scooping him into her arms. She cradled his head against her breasts. "I did, but that doesn't mean you have to marry me."

"You haven't answered my question."

She rocked gently, considering his dark blue eyes. "Can I think about it?"

"I'll give you two minutes."

She frowned at his ultimatum. "Hmmm, you're not going to make this easy for me, are you?"

He shook his head. "One minute."

"Boy, talk about pressure," she quipped nervously. "Be serious. This is the rest of our lives we're talking about."

"Thirty seconds."

"If I decline?"

"Then you can find someone else to fix your boat."

Her eyes widened. "You do fight dirty. Okay, why not? Let's do it. But I'm going to tell the kids how you twisted my arm. Wait a minute; you do want children, right?"

"A passel. A dynasty."

CHAPTER SIXTEEN

"Rose took that well," Sabrina said, looking out the window, studying topography that swung back and forth from forested mountainsides to rolling farms with corn fields. They were on the highway heading back to Rhode Island and the Zephyrus.

Jay didn't respond as he focused on changing lanes. Although traffic was light on I-80, he refused to relax. Too many yellow signs warned of stray deer. So far, he hadn't seen any but the too-frequent cautions made his jaw clench. The man who once dared ocean crossings on small, leaky sailboats was nervous about deer. In his mind's eye, he saw the huge Cadillac plow through a herd, their bodies exploding, just like the carcasses he'd seen along the highway. He shuddered involuntarily.

Sabrina noticed. "Are you okay?" She placed a concerned hand on his thigh.

He nodded curtly, refusing to look away. Instead, he scanned the sides of the roadway. He swung the large car around yet another mangled corpse and couldn't resist a quick glance. Sabrina saw panic in his eyes.

"Deer don't generally wander onto the road during the day. They mainly come out at dawn and dusk, when it's time to feed," she said, casually adding, "We probably won't see any."

After two hours of silent, tension-filled driving, they neared the state line where Pennsylvania gave way to New York. Before they crossed the Delaware River, they stopped at the small town of Matamoras to stretch their legs and use the facilities.

At the rest stop, Sabrina fed dollar bills into a soda machine. She looked over her shoulder as Jay stepped out of the men's room. "Do you want something to drink?" Not waiting for a response, she fed another dollar into the machine. "Water? Or soda?"

Jay ambled over to her, viewing the choices. He punched a button and waited for it to clunk down into the opening. Then he twisted the cap, released the carbon dioxide and drank thirstily. He tossed the empty bottle into a waste bin. He hadn't spoken a word except for the occasional grunt all morning.

Sabrina frowned, then opened her bottled water and drank. She stepped outside into the early afternoon sunshine and rested against the fender of the Caddy. Jay followed and pulled the keys from his jean's pocket.

He walked to her side and opened the door. Sabrina ignored him, calmly sipping water. He waited a few seconds then thumped the door shut. Not sure what to say, he stood silent and still.

Sabrina arched an eyebrow. "You know, if you're already regretting asking me to marry you, why don't you say so? Instead of giving me the silent treatment."

Jay looked right and then left, anywhere but at her. Probably checking for eyewitnesses, Sabrina thought.

He shoved his hands into his pockets and stepped closer, straddling her. He looked at his boots before looking into her eyes.

"I'm not regretting anything," he said huskily. "I don't want anything ... anyone ... to ruin it."

She understood now. "Anyone? As in Faye?"

He nodded, then pulled his hands out of his pocket and

slid them up and down her arms. In a conciliatory gesture, he tugged her into a loose embrace. Although it seemed as if he were comforting her, she knew he was asking for reassurance. For her promise that nothing Faye said would change the way she felt.

"She can be ... difficult," he warned.

Sabrina placed the water bottle on the hood, then curved her arms around his waist and caressed his back. Her cheek rested against his chest, the worn T-shirt soft against her skin. She closed her eyes and inhaled the delicious scent of soap and sweat. "You intoxicate me," she said, sniffing in appreciation. "If you think I'll let anyone get between me and this," she said, rubbing her cheek against his heart, "you have another think coming. I won't be intimidated. She doesn't scare me."

Jay tightened his arms. "She's demanding. Possessive."

Sabrina tipped her head back to consider his troubled eyes. "You belong to me now. How's that for possessive?" Her heart beat erratically at the claim and she prayed he wouldn't pull away.

He didn't. He smiled indulgently, then kissed her.

"Let's hit the road. We can be home in a few hours if we beat rush hour traffic."

But they didn't. Traffic built up as they neared Connecticut so they stopped for a late lunch in Danbury.

Sabrina ordered ravioli, the Italian restaurant's house special. "This is so good," she gushed. She speared a stuffed pasta shell and held it out for Jay to try.

While he chewed, he nodded thoughtfully. "Almost as good as mine, but I'm not sharing."

"I figured as much," she said, then aggressively snatched a slice of his gourmet pizza.

She bit into the slice and hummed. "We should stay here and wait for dinner."

"Need to get home," he said tersely.

She looked at him through lowered lashes. "By the way,

what will we do about living arrangements? I live in Maryland."

Jay shrugged as if it were not an obstacle. "Move in with me."

"Just like that?" She snapped her fingers.

He nodded warily.

Sabrina's expression hovered between careful consideration and cartoonish overplay. She scrunched her lips, rubbed her chin and rolled her eyes. Then her face relaxed and she looked at Jay.

"Okay." She stole another slice of his pizza. "There's lots of rich people in Rhode Island and I'm sure they'll want my financial advice."

CHAPTER SEVENTEEN

Faye paced the small kitchen, a cigarette smoldering between her claw-like fingers. Jay sat at the old Formica table and watched her, his face stern.

She stopped abruptly and turned to him. "I can't believe you'd betray us," she snarled.

"Grandma, there is no us. Only you and me. We're the only ones left."

"The family! Your grandfather. Your poor mother! All dead because of Rose Windham and now you're going to marry that whore!"

Jay stood, the chair falling in his haste. "She is not a whore."

"She's a whore! Just like her grandmother! I can't stand to look at you. Get out of here!" Her last words rose to a screech as she pointed towards the door, the forgotten cigarette dangling from her fingers. She angrily threw it into the kitchen sink, then picked up the closest thing -- a jelly jar -- and threw it at the wall. It shattered and strawberry jam slid down the plaster, puddling on the floor amid shards of glass.

Jay was familiar with her hysterics. From the age of twelve, when his mother killed herself overdosing on heroin, he'd lived with Faye, endured her volatile temper, her rages, her insanity. At sixteen, he ran away and learned how to support himself. He found ways to make money, crewing on yachts out of Newport during the summer and working construction during the winter. He earned his high school diploma at night school and put himself through college.

He knew her anger would escalate, that more household items would crash and break around him. It's why she chose to live in the same old house, ignoring the constant state of disrepair. She surrounded herself with cheap, pitiful belongings that she could destroy at will. She refused to become attached to anything or anyone. Except Jay.

Now a man, he was the image of his grandfather. Tall, auburn hair, insolent gray-blue eyes, his freckles nearly obliterated by the sailor's tan. And just like his grandfather, he was leaving her for a Windham whore. She howled in frustration and opened a cabinet door. Skinny claws hooked around drinking glasses and she slammed them to the floor.

Jay stalked out of the house and headed for his truck. Faye would break and bash as long as he remained, almost as if she did it for him. He drove down the long, dirt driveway, leaving the decrepit bungalow in his rear-view window.

Inside, Faye heard the truck's engine roar to life, wheels spin. She plunged her fingers through her lank, gray hair and screeched. Slumping against the sink cabinet, she slid to the floor, wrapped her bony arms around her knees and cried, great, heart-wrenching sobs of fury. He was gone.

Jay couldn't go back to the loft. Couldn't face the tenderness and concern he knew he would find in Sabrina's arms. He didn't deserve it. Once again, he hurt his grandmother. He parked at Maude's and went inside the welcoming dark bar.

He sat on a stool and ordered a draft.

Maude ambled through the dining room, a stained apron encircling her large waist, a damp dishcloth tossed carelessly over one shoulder. She paused at the bar and looked at Jay.

"Little early to be drinking, isn't it?"

Jay raised his head at her gruff words. He didn't answer; just lifted the heavy glass mug and drank.

Maude moved a little closer, peering in the dark at Jay's hair. "What you been doing?" She raised a hand and brushed his head. Jay jerked back involuntarily. "You're covered in glass."

"It's nothing," he growled.

Maude stared steadily, then nodded. Hummmph. That dink grandmother of his was on another rampage.

Everyone knew about Faye's temper and destructive ways. Not only had the townsfolk called the law on her, but some suggested the boy be removed for his own protection. But the boy took care of that himself, running away from home. Why he ever came back, why he continued to put up with the insane old woman, nobody knew. But he had and he kept her house from falling on her head, despite her. He replaced the dishes and the furniture she broke, paid all her utilities, and had groceries delivered so she wouldn't have to go into town.

And still, she treated him the same way she treated her husband before the fire took his life. Same way she treated her daughter. Nobody was surprised when the forlorn girl grew into a rebellious teen and sank into a world of drugs. It was her only escape.

The entire town knew Faye West was batty, and they kept their distance. The only one who couldn't seem to accept it was her grandson. Still loyal despite her abuse.

Maude barked at the barkeep. "Get him the usual." Turning towards Jay she said, "If you're going to drink, and it looks like you're here for a while, least you can do is eat something."

Then she ambled away, pushing through the swinging kitchen door.

Sabrina paced the small apartment. Occasionally, she pulled the cell phone from her pocket, checking to see if she had somehow missed his call. She punched in his cell phone number and listened to it ring. It went to voice mail. "Where are you? Are you all right? Please call me."

They arrived in Warren late the night before and went straight to bed. Wrapped in each other's arms, they whispered stories from their childhoods. Some were funny, most were sad, but at least they talked. Something they had forgotten to do much of the past week.

"This is insane," Sabrina said, her voice hushed in the dark. "We've known each less than two weeks." She rolled to her side, looking at his profile. "Tell me this isn't insane."

"Believe me," he assured her. "I know insane and this isn't it." He curled a hand around her neck and pulled her mouth to his.

In the morning, she hid under the covers and pretended to sleep, hoping he would make coffee. He did, then brought a cup into the bedroom. Leaning against the built-in dresser, he sipped. "I know you're faking," he informed her.

Sabrina pulled the sheets down and sniffed. "Did you make me a cup?"

He gestured towards the door with his coffee cup. "Nope. Going to have to get up, get it yourself." Then he settled back and watched as she stretched, climbed out of bed and searched for her panties. Giving up, she picked up one of his T-shirts, smelled it, then shrugged. She pulled it on and it fell to her knees. Walking past him, she spotted her underwear. "Oh, there they are." She plucked them from the windowsill and stepped into them.

She nodded towards the kitchen. "Okay, show's over.

Let's eat breakfast."

Once she settled with a cup of coffee, she looked through cabinets and the refrigerator, peering into the bright, nearly empty cavern. "I think we have the makings for omelets," she said, pulling out a plastic bin of cheese and smelling it. She put it on the counter behind her and extracted a carton of eggs and a container of butter. In the cabinets, she found a can of ham and a small container of sliced mushrooms. "Ta-da!"

"Tell you what, Merlin. You magically make breakfast; I'll go take a quick shower," Jay said.

"Fine, but eggs cook quickly. You better be out here in five minutes or I'm starting without you." Her stomach growled.

True to his word, he was back and at the counter before the omelets finished cooking. Sabrina placed the morning paper next to his plate, minus the comics. They ate in companionable silence, each reading the newspaper. It felt right.

Behind the paper, Jay spoke. "I'm going to see Faye this morning."

Sabrina felt her stomach knot. "Do you want me to go with you?"

"No!"

She felt relief at his abrupt refusal. "Okay then, I'll just stay here. Maybe do a little cleaning. Guess I'll make a grocery list. I need to call Rose anyway and let her know we're in."

A noise beneath the floor startled her. "What's that?"

"It's Brett. Today's a workday, sweetheart."

Sabrina smiled. "Of course."

Jay dropped the paper and stood. "Thanks. That was excellent." He picked up his truck keys and wallet, sliding them into his pocket. He leaned over the counter and kissed her lightly. "I'll be back soon. Then we'll go to the store. Going to need more than groceries."

Whistling, he walked out the door. Sabrina watched

from the window as he trundled down the stairs. He paused at the yawning opening of the boatyard shop to talk to Brett. He gestured to the apartment and Brett looked up. Sabrina waved. Then the heavy-set man playfully punched Jay in the arm. He turned back to the window, his hands clasped to his heart. She heard his faint call. "It should have been me! I'm the one who saw you first."

Jay slid his hands in his back pockets, watching Brett kiss his fingers to the lovely woman in the window. "Alright, stuff it or I'll tell Shawna. Better yet, I'll tell Maude," he said. Then he turned and looked into the shop. The Zephyrus sat upright, supported by two-by-fours. The boat, once a source of torment, was only a pitiful shell. He winced and recalled all the years he'd agonized over it until Sabrina's soft touch lifted the curse. Now, it was easy to let the anger go.

With his eyes steady on the fiberglass hull, he said, "Brett, take off. You've been carrying the shop alone and you deserve some time."

"I don't mind," Brett said.

Jay glanced over his shoulder. "Ayuh, but I do."

Brett nodded. "Okey dokey, you want me to go fishing again, right?"

"Unless you want to go home."

Brett walked into the shop and turned off the fans and lights. "I think I will, brother. You've inspired me."

That was hours ago and still Jay hadn't returned. Sabrina killed time taking a shower, cleaning the apartment and making lists. She couldn't wait any longer. Something had to be wrong. She started to pull on her shoes when she heard a noise downstairs. It'd been quiet for hours. She assumed that Brett had left for an appointment. She heard more bangs and a crash.

Jay must be back, she thought.

She stepped to the window, looked outside but did not see the truck. She went into the bedroom, stood on the bed and peeked out the high window. No trucks out front either. Then she heard his footsteps on the stairs. She hurried into the living room and swung open the door.

"Thank goodness, you're back. I've been so worried …" her voice trailed off. Stepping through the opening was a thin, wizened woman. She had both shaking hands wrapped around a gun. "Get back," she said, snarling.

Startled, Sabrina backed up raising her palms in supplication. "Who are you?"

The woman advanced, pushing the door closed with her bony hip. She leaned back against the door and reached one hand behind her to lock it. "You whore," she spat. "Think you can steal my grandson?"

"Faye?"

"You call me Mrs. West; you piece of trash!"

Sabrina lowered her hands and took a step forward. "Mrs. West, what are you doing?" she said, her eyes pinned on the gun.

Faye cradled the hand holding the gun and raised it. "Don't come any closer." She nodded towards the sofa. "Sit down."

When Sabrina didn't move, Faye pointed the gun at the ceiling and pulled the trigger. A bullet drove into the plaster and white flakes fell like snow. "Now!" she screeched.

Half a mile down the road, Jay lifted his head. He looked at the bartender. "Did you hear that?"

The man shrugged. "Nah, what was it?"

Jay swiveled on the stool. "Sounded like gun fire. Who could be shooting a gun in town?" He slid off the seat and headed for the tavern door. He opened it and looked cautiously outside. Then he lifted his head and smelled it. Fire! Not just fire, but burning resin. He called over his shoulder. "Call the Jakes! The boatyard is on fire!" Then he raced out into the sunlight.

Sabrina covered her nose at the stench. "What is that smell?"

Faye grinned wickedly. "That's your death you smell, whore. This time you're not getting away."

Sabrina was confused. "What are you talking about?" Then she gagged on the fumes. Smoke drifted in the cracks and ductwork. "Oh my lord! The shop is on fire! We have to get out of here."

She stood and stepped towards Faye, grabbing the old woman's tiny arm. "We've got to leave now."

Faye snatched her arm back and screeched. "Not this time, bitch. There's no one here to drag you out." Then she swung her hand, hitting Sabrina on the side of the face with the gun. Sabrina sank to her knees, covering her head as the woman battered her again and again.

"Please stop!" she cried. "You don't know what you're doing." If there had been an opportunity to stop the woman's assault, she missed it. Never considering the woman would hit her or that she knew about the fire, Sabrina's only concern was to pull her from danger.

"I know exactly what I'm doing," Faye growled. "You're not going to get him. He belongs to me."

Footsteps pounded up the steps outside and frantic hands turned the doorknob. When it wouldn't open, Jay began thundering on the wood. "Sabrina, get out of there! The shop is on fire!"

The old woman backed up and once again raised the gun. Sabrina looked up, blood streaming down her face and mixing with tears.

"Why have you done this?" she cried.

Jay turned the knob again. He heard voices. Women's voices. Pounding on the door again he begged, "Sabrina, for God's sake, open the door!"

He backed up and slammed into the door. It held,

144

bruising his shoulder. Then he kicked at the knob. He kicked several more times, the wood at the latch starting to splinter.

Two more kicks and the door burst open. Horrified, he saw Faye West standing over Sabrina, a gun pointed at her head.

"You thought I would let you get away, but you were wrong!"

"Grandma, put the gun down." He choked on the words. "We need to get out of here. The place is on fire."

Faye lifted her sharp, pointed chin. "I know. I started it. Just like before. When your granddaddy ran off with that whore. I knew about it. I knew all along. He didn't fool me. I knew he was running around behind my back. I just didn't know who with." She looked down at Sabrina's dark hair. "But I found out and then I told Don all about it. I was there that night. I watched them fight over her. He only cared about that whore, not his own wife. Or his daughter. It was all about her. But I was there. I knocked over the paint can. I started the fire, then I hit that bitch with all my might." Faye raised the gun to strike Sabrina again.

Jay stepped into the room. "No!"

Faye looked into his face, her eyes blazing. "But Don had to save her and in the end, they both died."

Jay moved closer to Faye. "Look at me, Grandma. Put the gun down. We have to get out of here." He heard sirens as the fire truck arrived. He gestured towards Sabrina, frozen on her knees as smoke wound up the stairs and filled the room. "She's not to blame for what Rose did. You can't punish her. Give me the gun."

Faye looked at Sabrina, her eyes narrow slits. "All that money isn't going to save you now."

She pointed the gun in Sabrina's face and her finger squeezed the trigger. The bullet drove into the ceiling as Sabrina's fisted hands flew upward, knocking the gun away. She rose like an avenging angel and a deep war cry sounded in her throat.

Before she could launch herself onto Faye, strong arms wrapped around her waist and carried her to the door. Jay shielded Sabrina against his body as he hurtled down the burning stairs. He raced into the parking lot and a police car jerked to a stop, barely missing him. He saw an ambulance and motioned for it.

A uniformed technician jumped out with a medic bag in one hand. Jay thrust Sabrina into the young man's arms. "Take care of her. I have to get my grandmother out of there!"

Then he turned back towards the shop, but before he could reach them, the stairs collapsed. Faye stepped into the second floor opening and surveyed the boatyard. Strangely calm, her eyes flickered over the flashing red and blue lights. She watched the fire fighters with the Warren Volunteer Fire Department dousing flames in the shop and Sabrina collapsing to the grass as a medic gently touched her face. And she saw Jay, hands fisted at this side, tears of frustration running down his face. She still held the gun, oblivious to the flames licking the walls around her. She lifted it, pointing it towards Sabrina. She could still do it.

"Grandma, no!" Jay looked helplessly around. "Somebody help! I need a ladder."

Fire fighters stepped back from the inferno in the boat shop and looked to the top of the building. One climbed up the fire truck and into the cherry picker. He flipped controls and the mechanical arm lifted the bucket to the building, hovering at the burning doorway.

Faye shook her head slowly and backed into the flames. Seconds later, a shot rang out and the top floor collapsed into the inferno.

CHAPTER EIGHTEEN

Sabrina sat on a gurney in a private treatment room at
St. Anne's Hospital. The doctor, a cheerful, balding
man in his mid-forties, pushed his glasses up his
nose. "You're going to have a couple of black eyes and a
bit of swelling," he said.

She raised a tentative hand to her head, wincing as her
bruised, splinted fingers brushed the bandages.

The doctor grinned apologetically. "Yes, you fractured
your hand when you knocked away the gun. That's going
to take a while to heal, also. Overall, you're okay. Just a bit
banged up."

Jay hovered behind the cot, one calming hand resting
on Sabrina's shoulder while he wiped his face with the
other. He smelled of smoke and antiseptic, having singed
his arms when he carried Sabrina from the burning loft.
He refused to leave her side, however, so a nurse supplied
him with ointment until he sought treatment.

The doctor glanced at Jay, and his expression turned to
one of regret. "I'm very sorry for your loss, Mr. West. If
it's any consolation, you should know that your
grandmother didn't suffer in the fire. She died instantly."

Jay nodded quickly, and turned his head. He didn't

want to talk about Faye. Didn't want to remember the final gunshot.

The doctor stood and rolled the black, padded stool away from the bedside. He placed a clipboard with Sabrina's chart on the hospital table and looked out the sliding glass doors of the exam room. He gave Jay a minute to collect himself, to blink away the threatening tears.

He'd been on his feet, answering the questions of police and fire officials during the hours since the fire and Faye's death. He still reeled from the implications, from the truth: Faye West had killed her own husband and Don Windham, and tried to murder Rose Windham, also. She set the fire at the West Wind Boatyard all those years ago. Consumed by bitterness and jealousy, she'd ruined her daughter's life, and very nearly Jay's life. She nearly succeeded in killing Sabrina, as well.

He'd underestimated her anger, the depth of her hatred and the insanity that accompanied it. A part of him cringed at the horror she'd become, but another part mourned for the lonely, unhappy woman. Unbidden, silent tears slipped down his cheeks. He turned his head and swiped at them with his forearm. The room's occupants faded, Sabrina's questions and the doctor's answers becoming a distant murmur.

A timid knock on the glass partition broke his reverie and he looked into Brett Story's loyal, sympathetic face. Brett lifted his chin, a manly show of support. Jay heaved a deep sigh, his lips flattening into a grimace. Then his eyes softened as he watched his best friend nod toward the blue chairs in the waiting room, indicating he'd wait nearby.

"Jay?" Sabrina's voice was low and raspy, her throat still raw from the smoke. "Jay," she repeated as she stood. "We can go home now."

Jay's gaze fell to her face and he flinched at the sight of her bruises and injury. The nurse had shaved long, dark hair from the left side of her head to accommodate rows of stitches. Mournful, he shook his head. They had no home. It had gone up in flames.

Sabrina understood and slowly blinked. "No, not home. I mean, we can go now. To a hotel, if that's okay?"

She swayed into his embrace, her voice muffled against his chest. "I'm very tired," she whispered. "I just want to lie down. Feel your arms around me."

Four days later, Faye West's cremated remains were placed in St. Mary of the Bay Cemetery. An outcast in life, death found her with no friends to mourn her passing. None except Jay West, with Sabrina on one side and Brett on the other.

Temporarily out of work, Brett would oversee the cleanup of the burned boatyard while Jay accompanied Sabrina to Eaton. She wished she could wait until the stitches were removed, but she needed to return to Rose.

Once again, the couple drove to the Pennsylvania town. They arrived at the hospital as visiting hours wound down.

Sabrina didn't want to horrify Rose, so she wore a scarf to hide her injury. Still, her grandmother's broken sobs hurt worse than her bruises. She clasped the woman's frail hands and shushed her.

"I'm fine, Grandmother. It's over," she said, laying her head on the bed.

"To think, all those years ago, she was there. That she started the fire." Rose's words were barely audible over the ambient noise of the hospital. "And she hurt you. Tried to kill you. My darling, precious girl." She pulled a hand free from Sabrina's and cupped her chin.

Then she raised her other hand and reached imploringly. Jay stepped to the bedside and held it.

"Thank you. Thank you for saving her," she whispered, tears spilling again from her blue eyes. She pulled his hand down to the bed and laid it atop Sabrina's. "It's time everyone stopped paying for my mistakes. You need to start your lives free from all misery I've caused."

Sabrina shook her head. "Grandmother, Faye had a choice. She didn't have to start the fire or attack you. She knew you were there to break up with Derek. But she wanted revenge and it destroyed her."

Sabrina glanced up at Jay. "There's a proverb that says, 'Before you embark on a journey of revenge, dig two graves.' Faye dug one for us all."

She bowed her head. "Even the Zephyrus is gone."

"Not exactly," Jay said. He pulled a small bronze plate from his back pocket and read aloud, "Zephyrus 32, No. 1, Zephyrus Yachts, Warren, Rhode Island."

He gently tugged on her hand until she stood beside him. "Let me explain something about boats. They're never gone. Little by little, if she's around long enough, everything gets replaced. Except one thing," he added, putting the builder's plate in her hand. "Let's restore what's missing. I need a boatyard and West Wind is a great name for a new business."

Sabrina wrapped her arms around his waist, her eyes shining. "I suppose, with a bit of luck, we'll be sailing a Zephyrus?"

Jay grinned. "Who needs luck? We've got destiny."

THE END

ABOUT THE AUTHOR

Robin Van Auken is an author with more than a dozen published books, including contemporary adventure, thriller and romance novels.

She and her husband enjoy traveling to the United Kingdom and Europe, and spend much of their time abroad in ruins, castles, cathedrals and museums. She particularly enjoys crypts with mummies, musty libraries and authentic pubs. In the United States, they bounce along the East Coast, traveling from New England to Florida to visit family and friends.

Robin's books include elements of her passions: traveling, boating, scuba diving, hiking, history and archaeology. The characters in her novels have a connection with idyllic Eaton, a fictitious town in Pennsylvania she invented, although many of her books also feature exciting and exotic cities the heroines (and their lovers) visit during the course of their romantic journey.